The Vial So Precious

Vangie Reeves

WESTBOW
PRESS®
A DIVISION OF THOMAS NELSON
& ZONDERVAN

WestBow Press books may be ordered through booksellers or by contacting:

WestBow Press
A Division of Thomas Nelson & Zondervan
1663 Liberty Drive
Bloomington, IN 47403
www.westbowpress.com
1 (866) 928-1240

ISBN: 978-1-9736-2098-3 (sc)
ISBN: 978-1-9736-2099-0 (hc)
ISBN: 978-1-9736-2097-6 (e)

Library of Congress Control Number: 2018902259

Print information available on the last page.

WestBow Press rev. date: 02/27/2018

This book is dedicated to Ken Reeves (Vangie) 1954-2002,
who first told me the good news of Jesus Christ and the story
of Agar Barshoman as told by Johna Reeves Platero

Ken [Vangie] was a great story-teller and enjoyed telling the story of Agar to his wife during her months of incarceration. Vangie died in 2002 from HIV/AIDS and his wife, Johna, has now written the story to share with you. She resides in Neosho, MO with her faithful Golden Retriever and husband. Her sisters, Mary McCreery and Valerie Ball, worked with her in the development of this story and the upcoming story: *Agar's Diary.*

Valerie Ball loves the scriptures and has used her creative talents to illustrate this story. She is happiest sketching, gardening, and raising bees on her farm in rural Missouri.

Chapter I

"My God, my God why hast thou forsaken me?" Darkness enveloped the crowd of onlookers, the hill called Golgotha, the cross, and the man upon it from whom the cry had come. A chilly dampness was in the air, the kind that clings to you, causing those in attendance to shiver and draw their robes more tightly about themselves. The dying man, or men to be exact for there were three, were a sorry lot to behold at the best of times and these were not, at least for them, the best of times. The three hung on separate crosses stationed several paces apart, about forty feet, and were in various stages of death. There is a cruelty within man that causes him to so unashamedly exact the price of another's life and to do so publicly. It is the same force that brings curious onlookers to such a display and thus many in attendance did not know any of the principals.

Two of the crucified, the ones on the left and the right were thieves, criminals of habit and or sordid reputations, deserving, at least by Roman law, of this awful fate. The man hanging on the center cross, the one who had cried out, was neither a thief nor a criminal. He was tried and that unjustly for one reason only; He had said he was the Son of God.

One stood among the inquisitive crowd gathered there and hearing these words he shuddered, the hairs of his arms and neck standing on end. John felt so crushed, so very much alone, so afraid.

John, the son of Zebedee, was a strong man of medium height and built with shoulder-length hair dark like oiled walnut. He wore a beard, as did most Jews of that day, that framed his face in such a way that it softened his features causing John to look almost boyish. His eyes were brown, but lighter than his hair and beard, more the color of caramel, and were normally graced with just a hint of humor. John's eyes softened his appearance and upon first meeting him they helped to relax even the most standoffish of people. These eyes now though were filled with hurt and confusion. John's right arm was around the shoulders of a slight woman, always small but seeming frail and weak as he had never seen her. She sobbed uncontrollably and though he did what he could to console her, John knew that Mary would have no peace this day, nay and for many to come as well.

Mary, the mother of the crucified Jesus, could not look upon her eldest son. It was not because of shame, but because this, her child, was barely recognizable even to her. As earlier John, the son of Zebedee, had held tightly to her just as he was doing now, and it was all that kept her from trying to halt the destruction of her son.

Mary and John

Always Jesus had been special to his mother, not because he was her firstborn but because He was the Son of God. Mary had always known this truth; however, she didn't begin to comprehend the weight of it or the terrible price that Jesus would one day pay. If she had understood, if she could have foreseen what they would do to her child, Mary would have fled all Judea. She would have hidden Him from the horrible evil that had befallen Him. She would have kept Him from His destiny.

Laughter could be heard coming from the irreverent scoffers that openly mocked the dying man. Many of whom only days before had listened to His teachings, hailed Him as King crying out, "Hosanna, hosanna to the King" as Christ had entered this city on a donkey. This city destroyed Him. John surveyed the pain etched face of Jesus hoping for some sign that God had not truly forsaken him, nor forsaken them all. Everything John believed in, all his hopes and dreams were nailed to the cross along with his Lord. Christ's promise of a kingdom, of a new Jerusalem, a new heaven and a new earth, His words of peace and love; everything He taught, everything they all stood for, and now? John had no answers only questions. He shuddered involuntarily as he realized that there was no one now to answer the many uncertainties. For there before him; pierced and bleeding, stretched upon a gruesome cross was the Master. John, called a son of thunder by the Lord and also called beloved by Him, beheld his friend and wept. The inexplicable madness of it all eluded John. It made no sense. This precious Man was now dying, beaten so profoundly, pierced with spikes and stripped of both apparel and dignity, and why? Maybe he was dying because He spoke of a better world, a place of peace and understanding, a place of love. Jesus hung as a common criminal between two felons. Ah, but He was far from common, never so. And he was not only unlike these fellow sufferers; Jesus was unlike any man John had ever known. In all the time John had spent with the Master, and it was considerable, he had witnessed not one act of injustice; not one unkindness on Jesus part. Never had the Lord caused another pain or suffering, to the contrary He had eased these things. Still here He was, the Master now near to dying, abandoned. He was abandoned not only by this wicked crowd, but by

His people as well. His family save Mary was not here, His disciples who had once left all to be with Him were not present either except for John.

"My God, my God why hast thou forsaken me?" The words echoed in John's mind dulling his senses. An awareness grew that Jesus had likewise been abandoned by His God. Oh, my Lord John thought, if only you would have heeded our warnings when we compelled you to avoid returning to Jerusalem. If only you would have reasoned with the priest or responded to Pilate's interrogation.

"The Nazarene saved others yet cannot save Himself." Someone shouted and many laughed encouragements.

In John's grasp Mary shook with grief and the beloved disciple clutched her closer to himself trying to shield her from the taunts and ridicule. Noting the faces of those near to him John was resigned to seek them out later and exact a price from them for their jeering. At the same time, he knew that he would not, he could not for it was not in keeping with the Lord's teachings.

Then as if echoing John's thoughts Jesus cried out once again, "Father! Forgive them; they know not what they do."

John silently plead with Christ, "Lord for your sake, for Your mother's and for ours, save what remains of your life." But he also knew that Jesus would not for by his own words even God was not listening. How could John possibly understand the drama that was unfolding? Even the prince of darkness did not know of God's great plan of redemption or realize the magnitude of the mistake he'd made in crucifying the Christ. Nor did Satan know that the war between good and evil was not yet over.

A short distance away from where John stood with Mary another pair of eyes watched the dying Man. Agar Barshoman; a greedy uncultured little man stared fixedly at this Jesus called the Christ. He was not sickened by the swollen appearance of Jesus features, the bruises already blackening the punctures of His brow oozing multi-shades of blood into His eyes, down His ears, cheek and neck. Nor was the massive amount of blood that covered Christ's torso and limbs appalling, rather Agar Barshoman found it fascinating.

Obviously, Agar was not a follower of this Rabbi, that is to say he did not adhere to the teachings of the Nazarene. Howbeit Agar did follow the career of Jesus and was enthralled by His rise to popularity which was unparalleled. Certainly, there were many would-be prophets and zealots prior to this Man, but none who had endeared the people like this Nazarene. Jesus was unique. The substance of His message went beyond mere anarchy. Absent also was the malice toward the Roman rule, as well as hostilities directed at the Jewish leadership, or lack thereof. The theme of Jesus message was more basic.

Jesus talked of a need to return to love and peace, a way of life that sustained itself by helping others, meeting needs and extending mercy to your fellow man. Giving and not taking, of meekness and not reprisals motivated by anger at injustice. Unique was Jesus too in that He lived the way He talked. The words He used, and statements of His beliefs were not merely words; they were applied to Christ's life and habits. It was said He had healed the sick, met the needs of many, and even raised the dead. No wonder, mused Agar Barshoman, the people adored Him. Agar knew for a fact that the crowd calling for Jesus death was not representative of the true regard most held for the Man. He knew because he himself had been among them and had been paid in silver for so doing.

"Crucify Him, crucify Him, away with this Man. Give us instead Barabbas," had been the solicited response when asked by Pilate what the fate of the Nazarene should be. Agar smiled. Barabbas. This one knew well enough to wager that though spared this time Barabbas hour upon the cross would come. Agar was certain that Barabbas' vile temper would assure it.

Agar Barshoman withdrew from his tunic pocket the item he had been absentmindedly fondling. It was a medium size vial, about six inches long and an inch or so in diameter. Slowly he removed the cork stopper from its mouth and rolled the vial back and forth in his hand. Agar's nearly black eyes searched for the nearest of the Roman soldiers and was pleased as he watched them huddled on the ground apparently casting lots for some of Jesus belongings.

Agar with Vial and Soldiers

Evidently, they too recognized the Nazarene's worth. Agar chuckled softly. After scrutiny of those around him Agar felt calm that no one was more than abstractly attentive to the crucified Man now nearly three hours into this drawn out form of death. Even the priests who had initiated the murder of the Nazarene were seemingly bored and loosing their prior zest for His suffering.

His heartbeat increasing only slightly, Agar quickly stepped from among the crowd of onlookers and approached the cross and person of Jesus. After one more look to be certain the soldiers had not yet noticed him Agar raised upon tiptoe and extended the open vial as far as he could reach placing it between the wood cross and the body of Christ. As he stood there watching, blood flowed into the vial and across the fingers that held it firmly in place. The warm fluid was dark and sticky and as Agar's dark eyes traced its course Jesus opened His own eyes and met the stare of Agar Barshoman!

Agar was so filled with fear he nearly released the vial and ran. He wanted suddenly to turn away, but his eyes were locked to those of Jesus. Agar felt completely exposed, more naked than the Nazarene, and knew somehow that this Man was searching his very heart and soul. Agar choked the urge to cry out, afraid that the soldiers would be alerted. Only Agar's greed overcame his fears and held the vial in place. Though it seemed like hours, the blood overflowed the vial in less than a moment.

Agar Barshoman turned away from the cross at last, capped the vial and fled on wobbly legs just as a Roman soldier shouted, "Get away from the cross or join Him on it."

Trembling Agar made his way through what remained of the crowd and disappeared into the shadows. Though quite shaken by the experience, Agar began to regain composure and was very pleased by his own cleverness. Leaving the scene quickly behind him Agar began to feel confident once more. Someone will pay a hefty price for the blood of the Christ. He laughed to himself as he made his way back to the city and to his home. What Agar Barshoman did not know was that the person who would pay the price would be him.

Chapter II

A KNOCK AT THE DOOR, THOUGH light, gained the instant attention by all the men within the room. Eyes searched the wood as if to penetrate the obscurity and peer beyond it and then turned in near unison to rest upon John. You could smell the fear that permeated the room, a peculiar odor at once strange yet unmistakable. And why not fear for their Master had only hours before been arrested, hastily tried, scourged and murdered. All of Jerusalem knew the men in this room to be disciples of the Christ and God alone was certain of their fate. As for John, he cared little and thought of himself ready to die in Christ's name and yet reflecting on the arrest and trial of his Lord John was saddened at the utter disregard for truth or justice. Everyone there knew that Jesus was innocent, even the governor Pilate had voiced the fact. Still mockingly, the false witnesses were brought forth and allowed to spiel their lies, lies presented as fact, lies they themselves could not agree upon. John, a fisherman, was not familiar with the intricacies of religious politics; therefore, would never understand why Jesus posed such a threat to the priests and rulers. Wasn't their concern the welfare of the people as was the Lord's? No, quite obviously it was not, for these self-proclaimed godly men connived and plotted, paid their evil bribes and finally even Pilate was turned against the Master thus turning Him over to be beaten and to be crucified. Oh, the horror of the scourging. One did not spend much time in Jerusalem these days without observing many such public floggings and all were awful, but with Jesus more so as the soldiers assigned the task went at it with a fervor John could not comprehend.

The zeal displayed in flaying the flesh from Jesus back, legs and even neck had been unparalleled. The Master's torso had been awash in crimson causing even the hardest of observers to avert their eyes from the gore. It proved, for John called the beloved, only the first of many times he would be unable to look upon his Lord that day. Yet as terrible as the beating had been it was the sounds that came from Jesus clenched teeth that John would never be able to forget. All through the trial Jesus had remained strangely silent, refusing to engage in the desired banter with the priests. These so called holy men had hoped to hear Him plead for His life, to crawl to them and grovel for their mercy. Instead the Master watched them fulfill their hateful deeds dispassionately and in so doing perhaps contributed to their universal anger. But when the cat-of-nine tails continually wrapped itself around Christ's torso separating flesh from muscle, blood flying in all directions exposing nerves and racking His tortured body with pain, Jesus had at last been unable to maintain His silence. Low guttural moans emerged, not man in tone but animal noises, half agony half anger, and completely torment.

Again, the rapping came, twice then quickly twice more and again the disciples gathered in the dimly lit room sought John's guidance. "Let them in," the son of Zebedee responded in answer to their searching looks.

Nathaniel rose and moved quietly toward the door. "Who is there," he whispered and visibly relaxed, as did the group gathered, when the voice of Philip was recognized. Nathaniel raised the locking bolt and slid it aside then pulled the heavy door ajar. After Philip quickly entered, Nathaniel closed the door and secured the lock once more, the bolt squeaking as he slid it into place.

Formal greetings were not exchanged, replaced instead by hushed salutations and nods as the eight disciples already gathered in the small room were anxious for news of what was happening outside in the streets and allies of Jerusalem. Along with John the beloved and Nathaniel there was James the brother of John, Matthew, Thaddeus,

Simon Zealot, Thomas and Andrew the brother of Simon Peter. Of Jesus twelve disciples only, James the son of Alphaeus and Peter were not in attendance, and of course Judas Iscariot the betrayer. It was with news of Judas that Philip now stood breathlessly before the rest.

"Judas is dead," Philip whispered when he was certain he had the whole of their attention. Gasps of disbelief and shock accompanied the announcement as he had anticipated, and Philip waited for the first of the many questions he knew would follow.

"Oh, my Lord," said Andrew softly as each man seemed to absorb Philip's words.

The silence was suddenly broken by an angry Simon Zealot, "God be praised," he hissed, "The dog!"

"He was an infidel and a traitor. Would that he was burned," Simon finished. All eyes looked in disbelief at him when this was said. According to their custom only the most hated of criminals were cremated, it was an unspeakable horror and thus the ultimate curse.

It was Thomas who this time spoke, "How Philip? Did Peter kill him?" Although it was unlikely, Thomas knew that Peter had loved their Lord completely and there was a time when the big fisherman would have done so without hesitation.

Before Philip could respond James, the elder said disgustedly, "Peter? His own sin is just as great. What right has he to accuse another?"

The others exchanged puzzled looks having no knowledge of the sin to which James now referred. John who had been present and who had confided to his brother about Peter's denial, just as Jesus had foretold, now silenced James with eyes of fire added sternly, "Hold your tongue James. You also have no reason to boast, nor do any one of us. Did not we all flee? If you've judgment against Peter, then declare so openly but do so in his presence."

James looked down at his hands. It was true as his brother said, they were all cowards. James was ashamed of his words now, and of his actions when Jesus was arrested when none of them so much as raised a hand to help their Master.

John's voice softened as he continued to speak, "We must not panic. Is this the way we honor the Lord's memory, squabbling as frightened children, allocating blame and accepting none ourselves? In truth none of us are guiltless. How can we now ask Jesus forgiveness? My brothers we must remain unified, together we will face whatever comes and we must not so easily cast aside the teachings of Jesus of Nazareth." Suddenly it seemed that the fear, anger and resentment which had only moments before filled the room was dissipated. Once again, these men were disciples, they were brothers and they were friends.

"Tell us Philip," Matthew said at last, "What has happened to Judas?"

Philip sighed deeply then replied, "He died by his own hand. Hanged they say. Judas preceded Jesus unto death."

Distinctly John the son of Zebedee recalled the words he'd once heard Jesus say. "The Son of Man goes as it was written concerning Him, but woe to that man by whom the Son of Man is betrayed. It would have been better for that man if he had never been born." At the time the disciples hadn't understood the warning but now Judas was, well...John's thoughts returned to the group and to the task before them.

"What of James?" John queried Philip further concerning the son of Alphaeus. "Do you know where he is?"

"Yes," Philip answered reassuringly, "Near the temple. James watches there for signs of movement against us." The final words trailed off and once again the disciples' faces could not mask their worry.

"And what of Simon Peter?" Has anyone seen him?" John asked.

Philip shook his head slowly from left to right, then looking first to John to let his eyes meet those of Andrew, and though Philip wished to allay Simon's younger brother's obvious concern he answered, "To my knowledge no one has seen him, not since the trial." Andrew let out a slow sigh as John again spoke.

"We must find him. I fear for Peter's well-being." It was a fact and John saw no reason to hide the truth. Of late too many feelings had been suppressed and John the beloved believed that if Jesus were here the Lord would not approve.

Softly Andrew spoke, "I know where Peter is, at least I think I do. I will go to him."

"Yes," answered John, the leadership now thrust upon him. "Yes Andrew, go to Simon Peter and bring him here. It is critical that we remain united. Together with Peter among us we will decide what we have to do."

This said Andrew stood and moved toward the door. John stood also and embracing Andrew quietly added, "Tell Simon our Lord's work requires him and perhaps now more than ever. Tell Peter it is time to fulfill his calling." Andrew offered a weak smile then unlocked the door and swinging it ajar he entered the darkness and was gone.

Again, the remaining disciples waited. They exchanged hopeful glances, a few shrugged as if to shed the feelings of increasing gloom, and the tiny room was once more filled with the air of uncertainty.

Chapter III

IT WAS EARLY, PRE-DAWN AND Jerusalem was quiet. At least as quiet as it got during the days of festivities and rowdiness. Thousands flocked to Jerusalem during Passover each year, to this so-called holy city which was home to Jew and to Gentile. Many other burgs, Bethlehem, Joppa, Caeserea, and Capernaum were represented and from even as far as Damascus they had come. The cultures were as varied as their dialects and trade. Occasional laughter could be heard coming from a woman of the street no doubt, but it was anybody's guess from which city she hailed. The prostitutes, though many, were but a slight percentage of this annual mecca for there were also pick-pockets, thieves and cutthroats, criminals of every sort. Hundreds of merchants and tradesmen too, many which would also steal you blind for a small profit, gathered in the streets and alleys like starved vultures each seeking to make or enhance their personal fortunes. And fortunes could be made for along with the infusion of rabble were thousands of common people, a life's savings in their pockets and each with a yen to experience the pleasures, forbidden and otherwise, of Jerusalem at Passover. It was a once in a lifetime trek for some and silver and wine flowed freely. Roman soldiers also were more in abundance then usual for Ceasar wanted to remind the Jews that Rome was the ultimate power, thus, he had ordered the display of force. Though the Jews called Herod king, all of Rome's vast empire mocked him and allowed Herod only limited governing power. To

Ceasar, as to most, King Herod for all his pretentious splendor was little more than a royally clad publican.

The air, cool and moist, was laced with the pungent odor of camel dung hanging in the slight breeze so that even the homes of the elite could not completely eradicate its presence. For this reason, an odd blend of a hundred different incenses also pierced the senses, the effect dizzying on one unaccustomed to a city the size and atmosphere of Jerusalem. Agar Barshoman could not sleep. He raised himself from the narrow cot and paced the floor of the dingy little room that was his home.

The home Agar had secured by blackmail, and he was fortunate to have during these very busy times. Agar had threatened to expose the innkeeper's penchant for withholding Roman taxes; thus, had been allowed this room to insure his silence. The room was small, about eight feet square at most and had no window save for a four by ten-inch opening toward the ceiling and above the single door. It was through this tiny slot that any air from the street was received; therefore, the room smelled musty and stale. There was a small earthen pot in one corner that smelled appropriately of urine and waste and in another corner, nearer the cot, was a pile of dirty clothing and two more pots though one of these was obviously broken. It was this innocent looking heap that Agar watched fixedly as he stalked back and forth his sandaled feet creating small clouds from the dirt covered floor as he did so. Beneath this pile the vial was hidden.

Vangie Reeves

Clothes and Clay pots

It was quite apparent that the little man was worried. His shoulders were hunched, and brow knit while behind his back his frail hands worked feverishly to hold the other still. This was certainly not the first of Agar's many plots to cause him consternation and such fervid pacing; however, normally it was the nervousness of planning or the hunger for the profit that caused the anxiousness. In this instance Agar Barshoman was unsure about the cause of the worry he felt.

The scheme had worked perfectly. Without any hindrance he had gotten the blood and made his escape, all that remained was to find a buyer which in this spiritually active, greed focused city would be simple. Despite this Agar found sleep impossible. It was the eyes, the eyes of the dying Man that troubled him; yet he would not accept this fact. Never had a man eyes like those of this Nazarene Agar was certain. Eyes that were so kind, so captivating and that seemed to penetrate and yes cleanse you. An involuntary shudder coursed through his fragile body and he dismissed the thought. He felt silly even thinking such things. Agar reasoned that the eyes were not truly so strange; after all, the Man was dying, was He not? And just how often had Agar been so close to one so very near death? In fact, Agar assured himself, it was logical that his own fear and excitement had added to the moment supplying mystery to the scene and making the eyes only unique in memory. There was however one large problem with this theory; Agar Barshoman knew he was a liar and he knew even now that he was lying to himself.

Nearing the pile of clothes Agar bent to sort them intent on retrieving the hidden vial to examine its contents more closely. Somehow though he could not force himself to pick the vial up once revealed, and instead studied it from what he judged to be a safe distance of a few feet. After all he justified, it wouldn't do to risk dropping and breaking the container thus voiding his opportunity at wealth and maybe even fame. This little vial could be worth perhaps a fortune if he found the proper buyer. Agar knew that some had thought this Nazarene to be the Messiah and though he dismissed this notion as preposterous, many did not.

Thinking back to the crucifixion Agar recalled that even then a few had voiced their belief when though it was only midday the sky turned dark. Later when near His final moments Jesus had cried out to God or to Elijah and the ground began to tremble someone had shouted, "Surely, He is God's Son," and again, "This was the Son of God!" At the time Agar considered only that the darkness was an ally to his treachery, but now he realized that it was indeed strange. Still it was ridiculous for this Man, nay for any man, to be God's Son.

Agar Barshoman would never understand the zealots and fanatics that flocked to these many prophets who were always cropping up preaching of a better life or a new form of religion. They came promising change and hope, but never delivered and were usually imprisoned, stoned or as had been this Jesus, crucified. Time and again Agar had seen it occur, and yet when a new prophet arose to take the last one's place a horde of followers would again believe this one to be the Savior. Agar considered all such followers sickeningly weak and seeing they refused to accept reality. In all his 41 years Agar had known but one savior and that was money. Only wealth could bring the sort of peace he sought. After all, when did God in any other form ever feed him or clothe him or calm his nerves?

Agar Barshoman replaced his soiled laundry atop the vial and stood grunting aloud as he did so as if he were dismissing all forms of piety once and for all from his mind. Let the priests and judges be his holy conscience, they were the most experienced were they not? And besides they trusted in his own god he thought, for he didn't know one of them that could not be bribed.

"I will buy my peace of mind," Agar said aloud to no one, then with a grin added, "And I will pay for it with blood."

Chapter IV

"ARE YOU QUITE CERTAIN CLEOPHUS? We want no mistake."
"Yes Annas, everything has been taken care of. We will have no more trouble with this rabble." Annas, an elder of the chief priest, paced nervously back and forth after hearing this remark. The terrace of his home was the setting for this latest conspiracy against the message and follower of Jesus and the beautifully kept flowers added to the irony of the scene. It was here in these peaceful surroundings that Jesus had been first condemned having been brought here from the garden of Gethsemane following the betrayal by Judas and the subsequent arrest. With Annas now was Cleophus Rex, a Roman centurion assigned to the temple guard, and he too had been present on that night. Cleophus was several years Annas' junior and did not share the concerns that plagued the old priest. Fear, the aged Cleophus felt was an ally, and it was with masked contempt that he viewed Annas.

Finally, the elder man stopped his pacing and considered the face of the soldier before him. After a moment he asked, "The men you have placed at the tomb then, they can be trusted?"

Annas noticed Cleophus' jaw muscles moved slightly at this query and he knew the younger man considered the question an insult. So be it, Annas thought and stated, "I must be absolutely certain."

Cleophus only forced a smile and answered flatly, "I have personally selected them lord priest and I give my word, there will

Vangie Reeves

be no mistake." Having said this Cleophus looked away and plucked a bright pink rose from a bush near him as if the subject was closed. He brought the tender flower to his nose and inhaled deeply closing his eyes as he did so.

Annas saw the act as one of defiance and thus prodded further, "Still, I have heard that this plan of Jesus' followers is well thought out. They will stop at nothing to trick the people into believing that this Nazarite dog is the Messiah, and if they succeed the Man's death will accomplish more than all his teachings ever could have. The body must not be removed." Annas stressed the final words and in so doing let Cleophus know that he alone would be held responsible.

The words angered the centurion and it was obvious as he glared at Annas and said, "I assure you, this so-called plan is merely a rumor and even if it were not, who would carry it out? The disciples of Jesus have scattered like frightened sheep, no one has seen them, and they have no one to lead them. For the most part Annas, they are fishermen and simple craftsmen. They would not dare challenge a Roman guard."

Cleophus sighed and continued, "The men I placed at the tomb are well prepared to prevent any molestation of the corpse. Annas these misfits have had their day. Jesus is dead, and His followers pose no threat."

Annas nodded his head as if to agree but did not rid his face of the scowl that made him look like a very sad camel. Ignoring Cleophus' attempt to pacify him Annas persisted, "And what of the big Galilean?" he asked referring to Simon Peter. "I am told he has fists of iron instead of flesh and bone."

Cleophus laughed and answered, "If you mean the one called Peter, it seems he also has a heart of cheese. He turned out to be the biggest coward of them all. He was seen crying in the courtyard like a professional mourner. Why even one of your handmaids will tell you that the big Galilean refused to admit even knowing he Nazarene. I'm told he cursed and denied every being a follower. No Annas, the fisherman is probably miles from here by now, fists of iron indeed!"

Cleophus turned away from Annas disgustedly and crushing the gentle rose he had been holding, he cast it to the ground. The younger man was sick of this nonsense. Let the old goat worry himself to death, what would it matter. Silently Cleophus was grateful that Caiaphas, the son-in-law of Annas, was the high priest at this time. The centurion was quite certain that Annas would never have the stomach for ridding them of Jesus. It was Caiaphas who had purchased the resources of Judas Iscariot, and he too that had convinced the Sanhedrin that crucifixion was necessary. Suddenly Cleophus remembered something that might change the course of the conversation and at the same time shock the elder priest.

"Did you know that two members of your own consul performed the burial of this Jesus?"

The announcement had the desired effect for Annas paled and barely whispered a reply, "You can't be serious Cleophus? Surely you are teasing an old man?"

"Nay, I would never think to do so dear, dear Annas," Cleophus responded walking over to the elder man and lacing his arm about the frail shoulders. It was apparent the centurion was enjoying the talk now and that he would make Annas ask before revealing the names of those involved.

Hoarsely, as if on cue, the priest did so, "Who, who are they?"

"Do you mean they never spoke of this with you?" Cleophus replied incredulously. "Why I assume it was under your instructions that they acted and to think these very old friends never mentioned it at all."

Again, Annas knew that Cleophus would say no more, so as was expected he said, "Who?" It was all he could force himself to say but to Cleophus it was payment enough for Annas' earlier insults.

Abandoning the mock affection, the soldier removed his arm from Annas and whirled about. As he strode defiantly toward the terrace gate he spat the answer over his squared shoulders, "It was Nicodemus I believe, yes and the one who received permission from Pilate was Joseph, Joseph of Arimathea."

Suddenly Cleophus was gone leaving Annas alone in the garden enclosure. The old man was unmistakably shocked by the revelation. Of all the members of the consul Sanhedrin Nicodemus and Joseph of Arimathea were two of the most highly respected and well-thought of.

"What could this mean?" Annas muttered this question over and over. Annas knew both men to be fair and peaceful. He knew that they often gave to the needy and that they were opposed to violence. Still for them to request and bury the body of this criminal made no sense. It was an act of open rebellion against the Sanhedrin itself. What was the motive for this defiance? Annas couldn't understand. Never once did it occur to the old priest that Nicodemus and Joseph might be followers of Jesus, and if it had Annas would have dismissed the notion as absurd for in his mind it was simply not possible. The old priest was suddenly very tired.

He was tired of this outlaw that found ways to trouble him even from the grave. Soon he promised himself, soon all memory of Jesus would fade into the past and disappear just like the stench of so many false prophets before Him. A few months hence and no one will remember that there ever was a man called Jesus of Nazareth. When would all these rebels and usurpers of deity cease to peddle their vain hypocrisies? And when, if ever, would the true Messiah come? Annas was plagued by many concerns but chiefly he must talk with Joseph and to Nicodemus about their involvement with the Man of Galilee. Surely, they were justified in risking the loss of respect from the consul and perhaps the loss of their very lives. Annas resolved to go to them and ascertain their reasons. If he was satisfied with their answers all would be well, but if not, well then, he would speak with Caiaphas, his near-son. The Sanhedrin elder felt a new surge of hope knowing that Caiaphas would have a solution. It was Caiaphas that had rid them of Jesus and his lot and Annas was satisfied that his son's-in-law judgments were so important that history would record his name forever. Leaving the quiet of the garden and entering his home the usually negative old priest was smiling while thinking aloud to himself, "Perhaps history will record my name as well." And with this thought Annas too became a prophet!

Chapter V

FOR NEARLY AN HOUR ANDREW watched the broad expanse of his brother's back. His presence had gone unnoticed as Andrew approached quietly and stayed a safe enough distance from Peter, a hundred yards or so, so that he would not disturb his brother's thoughts.

As the deep blue water lapped the shore Andrew was grateful for the tranquility of the moment and his thoughts retraced a scene he had once witnessed when with Jesus. The disciples were adrift one day when a storm came up suddenly and its ferocity threatened to sink the vessel. All on board were filled with terror save the Master who was sleeping in a lower part of the boat. In their panic they had gone to Jesus crying, "Lord we perish, save us."

Jesus was angry when He woke though it was not lack of sleep that troubled Him. What disturbed the Lord and what He scolded them for was their universal lack of faith. Andrew remembered that the disciples hadn't really understood their mentor until He stood in the bow of the ship and said, "Peace be still." Instantly the storm was quelled, and the sea was eerily calm. Watching the tumultuous waves, Andrew wondered what he might do to calm the storm raging inside Simon Peter. The two men were very close and had been always.

Andrew idolized Peter and was ever striving for his brother's approval. Simon Peter was the epitome of a man. He was six feet five inches tall and weighed about 230 pounds. He was strong from hoisting the great nets of his profession and muscles rippled at the slightest move he made. Peter's neck was nearly as thick as Andrew's thigh and his hands were large and vise-like. He was ruggedly handsome having a square chin, heavy-brow and a warm smile that was filled with confidence. Peter had thick wavy hair was as beautiful as any woman's it was dark as a raven's wing. His beard too was shiny black and accentuated the prominent cheek bones of his ancestry. Simon's emerald eyes flashed from beneath black bushy eyebrows where they defied any man to match their stare. Eyes that often danced with laughter but that could also appear threatening and cold. Few dared to challenge these eyes and even less the man. A golden ring encircled the lobe of Simon's left ear and added to the air of recklessness that clung to him. Andrew knew few men as imposing as his brother. Simon was a man that was all man. Watching him now Andrew could not believe this same man had denied their Lord; yet in fact it was true for Simon had told him directly.

After the trial but before the crucifixion his brother came to Andrew broken and sobbing, mumbling a confession of sorts about betraying Jesus publicly, about shaming the Master, declaring himself to be a coward. While Andrew tried to make sense of it Peter had pushed him away and disappeared into the night. Later Andrew sought John the beloved knowing he had been present at the trial and thus was told the details of the denial as John knew them.

Andrew inhaled a chest full of fresh sea air, felt the water's spray strike his face its salt stinging his cheeks. The younger man walked toward his brother and prayed for words to come. Andrew recalled when Simon and Jesus first met and everyone there knew the two unusual men had formed a bond at once. Andrew had been converted first by John the Baptist and regularly attended as the prophet spoke to vast crowds exhorting them to repent, to turn to God and be baptized. It was at one such sermon that Andrew first met Jesus. After John baptized Jesus in water the preacher turned to those near him and whispered, "Behold, the Lamb of God!"

Fascinated by the Baptist's appraisal, Andrew and another of John's faithful adherents began to follow Jesus, talking with Him and learning His ways. After awhile Andrew was convinced that

Jesus truly was the Messiah! In his excitement the young convert had rushed to Simon wanting him also to listen to Jesus speak.

"Simon, Simon you must come." Andrew had urged tugging on his brother's sleeve.

Simon only laughed and offered, 'What is it this time little brother? Has John Baptist flown off into a cloud?" Simon's booming laughter filled the air and Andrew too had laughed.

Andrew was often lovingly ridiculed by his brother, but after a few minutes, this time he said, "No Simon, listen to me. This is serious." After pausing for them to catch their breath and for Simon to realize his sincerity Andrew concluded, "Simon, we have found the Christ!"

Years had passed since that day and as Andrew now approached his brother he wondered, as he had wondered then, how Simon would react. "I thought I'd find you here," Andrew said.

Peter whirled about to face the voice and seeing Andrew he turned back to look out across the sea. "I want to be left alone," he answered. It was an order not a request.

Peter looking out to sea

"This is not possible Simon as you've no doubt already discovered. His memory will never leave us." Andrew realized that to speak these words he risked incurring his brother's wrath. He also realized that Simon had to let go of what had happened, that the future of them all was still at stake. Besides it would be better to take a beating if that was necessary than to have Simon torture himself as he had no doubt been doing.

The elder fisherman faced his sibling, but he responded almost as if allowing his thoughts to voice themselves; as if Andrew was not present. "Once I knew Him," Peter said, "Once not so long ago. It was at Caeserea Philippi and Jesus asked who the people thought he was. Some answered Elijah or John Baptist reincarnate, but I knew better. Then He asked what we ourselves thought. I saw this as my opportunity to declare my allegiance and I boldly said, 'Thou art the Christ, the Son of the living God,'" Simon's voice cracked, and he was silent.

After a moment Andrew said, "I remember Simon. Jesus called you Peter, the rock upon which He would build His church."

Simon Peter interrupted but still refused to look at his brother. "Once I knew Him Andrew, but not when He needed me, not when it truly mattered."

Andrew sighed then stepped up beside his huge sibling. "Jesus called you Peter and He called you blessed. He also called you friend. The thing you must remember my brother, the only thing, is that He called you."

Andrew paused then exhaled and continued, "You can't alter what is done, but you can become what Christ said you would be, the foundation of His church. Simon, we need you." The smaller man turned to Simon and with his eyes imploring him to listen added, "We cannot bring our Lord back, but we can see that His teachings are not forgotten. Jesus commanded us to continue and continue we must."

The tide steadily beat against the shore, sand soaking up the moisture from each wave, gulls squawked noisily above them, and the wind surrounded them rustling their cloaks causing a popping sound. In an embrace of love and unity the two brothers held one another tightly and wept.

An hour passed, then another and finally it was Simon Peter who spoke, "And the others Andrew, how can I face the others?" Peter realized that by this time half of Jerusalem knew of the denial, and among his fellow disciples his presence might not be wanted.

Andrew smiled reassuringly and replied, "Everyone wants you to come back Simon. John the beloved asked me to plead with you in their behalf. But truly he was most concerned about you personally."

Andrew looked into his brother's brilliantly green eyes, never had he seen them so sad, so full of remorse. "I will not lie to you Simon. Though no one else had any reason to point a finger, it will not be easy for you to face the rest. The sad truth is that some expected you to lay down your own life to protect the Lord. Well, what of it? You did not. What is done is done."

Listening to his brother's words, Simon Peter saw a new Andrew before him. The big fisherman stooped and picked up a flat rock from near the water's edge. Small waves of foam covered his feet and sandals as he did so. In a deliberate motion he drew his left arm back then suddenly flung it forward releasing the stone and causing it to skip across the surface dancing over waves several times before disappearing into the blue liquid.

Simon stood erect once more and though he physically towered over Andrew, he did not feel taller in his heart. The big Galilean shook his head fiercely as if to rid his mind of the last few days' events and looked at Andrew's gentle face. "To Jerusalem," Peter said and pointed in the direction they must travel, but he did not take a step until Andrew turned and led the way, then with his head bowed Simon Peter followed him.

Chapter VI

"ARRGH!" A SCREAM PIERCED THE silence of night, a scream filled with terror and pain. Joseph of Arimathea leaped from his kingly bed and scurried across an expanse of cold marble floor. In spite of near panic, he reached a mahogany night stand some 20 feet from where he slept nearly knocking a porcelain basin from atop it in his haste. Joseph never took time to study the reflection which peered back at him as he bent over the contents of his blue porcelain masterpiece. The reflection tainted the man's true image and gave him the pallor of the dead.

Grabbing a bar of soap also atop the stand Joseph began to meticulously scrub his hands and arms. His eyes were first wide open as if beholding horror of some type, then tightly shut apparently to close out the awful sight. After several minutes Joseph rinsed and re-rinsed so vigorously that water splashed upon his face, his chest and on the gray floor. The old man then picked up a dry towel from a stand beside the other, and though this stand was not as tall as the first it was equal in beauty and design and had obviously been fashioned by the same skilled hands. In fact, the stamp on each was the mark of one Joseph Bar Jacob, a craftsman now passed on, that Joseph of Arimathea had known well and highly respected. This same carpenter made the beautiful Lebanese cedar bed that Joseph of Arimathea slept on. He was the father of Jesus of Nazareth.

Joseph roughly dried himself, so much so that his already inflamed skin was near to bleeding. The Jewish elder opened his eyes at last to survey his accomplishments, "Arrgh," he exclaimed again and once more the scene was repeated. "Oh my God," Joseph cried, "Cleanse me, cleanse me that I might forget."

Vaguely Joseph wondered if Nicodemus was a party to this same nightmare. Silently he hoped his friend was not. It was the twelfth time, at least, that this drama had taken place since...since the burial of the Lord. Joseph had gone to Pilate and asked permission to inter Christ's body. Nicodemus had helped and since the time of the gruesome task poor Joseph had been unable to rid his mind of the sight of Jesus' corpse.

Absent from the scouring, and from the crucifixion also, Joseph had not been prepared for the shock of seeing his Master so completely destroyed. Joseph of Arimathea was an elder member of the Sanhedrin, as too was Nicodemus, though neither assented with the majority of the consul in demanding the death of Jesus. Both were in reality disciples of Christ though secretly for they feared reprisal from their colleagues had their allegiance been made public.

After Jesus death however, the desire for secrecy hadn't mattered. Joseph felt compelled to claim the body, to see to it that the Teacher had peace at least in death. Joseph of Arimathea forgot about his reputation and standing among his consul brethren, he sought and was granted the authority to tend to Jesus' remains. Joseph knew the Sanhedrin would summons him and demand he explain his deed. He expected too to be called a traitor to his position on the consul and Joseph decided it didn't matter, he would deal with their anger when it came. What Joseph didn't expect, what he couldn't possibly deal with was the condition of the Man he so dearly loved.

When Joseph of Arimathea first glimpsed the cross and Christ upon it he was driven to his knees in grief and shame. Jesus was barely recognizable, a mere form of blood covered tissue, swollen and blackening. "Dear God, if only I would have reasoned with them," Joseph's tortured mind screamed. "If Nicodemus and I had stood together and plead the Lord's cause perhaps we could have persuaded them, they might have listened, they might have released him." But they had not. Selfishly, in fear for their own safety, their own good standing, they had said nothing. They did nothing. And now? "Oh, my Lord," Joseph cried, "They have murdered You; they have destroyed You."

It had taken the better part of an hour for Joseph to regain enough composure to continue. Silently, numbly he and Nicodemus had removed Jesus' body from the wooden cross. Joseph knew that he would never forget the sickening sucking sound the spikes made when they had been removed. Nor would he ever be able to erase the image of the congealed blood that even when the nails were gone held the body to the coarse surface refusing to let it go, so much so in fact that they had literally been forced to pry the Lord's body from the cross. Never had Joseph seen so much blood. Blood was everywhere. From the top of Jesus' head to His pierced feet was blood, blood dark and sticky, wet and clinging. Eventually both Joseph and Nicodemus were drenched with it. It was the memory of the blood, the feel and smell of which Joseph could not free his mind.

Joseph had heard that Pilate, the governor, made a show of publicly washing his hands while declaring to the crowd, "I wash my hands of this innocent Man's blood."

Yet it was Pilate that handed Jesus over to be beaten and to be crucified, an indictment that would remain with him forever. Joseph stood in the semi-darkness of his bed chamber his head bowed and eyes awash with tears. "Would to God that I might wash my own hands of guilt," he sobbed, "And of the stain of the Master's blood."

Vangie Reeves

Chapter VII

I N ANOTHER PART OF JERUSALEM, a seamier violent part that was only a few miles from Joseph of Arimathea's lavish domicile in proximity but was generations away in culture and refinement, Hadid cocked one slender eyebrow and frowning studied the partially shrouded face of Agar Barshoman.

Hadid was a Bedowin merchant with harsh survival instincts common to the nomadic tribes of the desert. He was of Arabian descent and though he was not large in stature, he posed a very large threat as a foe in trade. His hair was thin and greasy, long strands fell loosely from atop his balding pate that shined from beneath like a dark crystal. His skin was the color of coffee and had been made leathery by long days in the sun. At this stage in his life, nearly 70 years, his wrinkles were deep and well-defined. His nearly black eyes twinkled giving the only clue to what he was currently thinking.

"The trouble with Agar," thought the older man, "Was that the Jew was a liar and a cheat." One could never be certain of Agar's facts or too careful in dealings which involved him.

Hadid watched Agar closely hoping to catch sight of a sign of nervousness or anything that would betray the younger man's intentions. What Agar offered was ridiculous Hadid thought, indeed, a vial of blood from the Messiah. Still, if it could be purchased cheaply enough a sure profit could be made, especially now at Passover season.

However, Hadid knew that Agar Barshoman would cheat his own mother, and had in fact.

"If you are telling me the truth," the Arab said aloud, "Which is unlikely, I might have an interest in the item you offer. But how are you going to prove the blood you claim to have is authentic? And, if I were to purchase it, which I doubt, how would I prove it?"

Agar Barshoman eyed the Arab merchant with only half-hearted interest. What Agar wanted to do was pull his hooded robe completely over his nose and mouth and close out the smell of the tent and of Hadid. The foul odor came from a mixture of body sweat, the Bedowin's unwashed clothing and the sickeningly sweet smell of opium to which Hadid was addicted. The elder man smiled through teeth that were few in number and badly stained from inhaled smoke and improper care. It was obvious to Agar that Hadid was enjoying his discomfort.

Silently Agar Barshoman cursed the vial which was the sole reason for this visit. Hadid had a reputation as large as his cherished desert. His dishonesty, it was said, was only exceeded by his shrewdness and it was the latter that appealed to Agar Barshoman. Agar knew that Hadid could not offer the price that the vial would ultimately fetch. However, the Arab could offer every argument against its purchase and this was knowledge Agar Barshoman could use to form the basis of his sales pitch for a true buyer.

Finally, Agar answered, "I can prove its origin two ways. First, I have a witness, one who saw the blood extracted and secondly, the vial itself has a mysterious power." Of course, neither of these was true, but Agar was curious to know Hadid's reaction.

He didn't have long to wait as Hadid snorted then laughingly mocked, "Your so-called witness is a liar, and the droppings of a donkey too has mysterious powers. I have no time for your foolishness, Agar Barshoman. Leave me, I am a businessman."

If the younger man had really left the tent as Hadid ordered the old man would have been both shocked and disappointed. His reply was merely part of a long-practiced custom of bartering. Make the other believe you weren't interested or even angry and you could often steal a treasure. It was a method Hadid had used many times and capitalized on again and again.

Agar Barshoman readjusted his legs beneath him angrily propping the grimy yellow pillow on which he sat. He coughed and pretended to spit in the dirt to his right doing his very best to appear insulted. Agar was amused by the old merchant. Surely the Bedowin must believe that Agar was an amateur at bartering to employ such a common trick. Quickly Agar reminded himself of Hadid's renowned for being shrewd, he must be careful not to take the Arab too lightly. If word spread that Agar Barshoman was easily duped he might lose his chance at a fortune.

Agar scowled and snapped his reply. "This is a very humble dwelling for one so extremely rich as you Hadid." Agar spread his arms wide and looked about the small tent. "I hadn't realized you were a seer as well as a successful, er, successful businessman." Agar smiled and returned his eye to those of the Arab before continuing, "Tell me Hadid is it often your mind leaves you this way?"

Hadid's dark eyes narrowed as his stare matched Agar Barshoman's. The old man reached for a small silken pouch next to his knee and hoisted it peeping inside momentarily. He withdrew a well used glad pipe from it and satisfied that the bowl was filled struck a match to light the opium within. The pipe glowed briefly and caused his fragile hands to warm as the opium ignited warming Hadid's lust for the drug. Now the real trading would begin he mused. He smiled inwardly knowing that this little Jew was grossly overmatched.

Hadid took his time again stoking the pipe while letting Agar wonder if his insults had the desired effect. Finally, Hadid responded, "Perhaps you would do me the kindness of explaining why I should believe your so-called witness." This might prove quite entertaining Hadid thought. He always enjoyed a master liar at work and Agar was known to be one of the very best.

Agar Barshoman was not always the vile person now seated before Hadid. Agar grew up in Jerusalem and as a young lad was very traditional in both upbringing and values. Jewish parents were usually quite strict, and Agar's were no exception. His father was a candle maker and worked long hours to meet the demands of a noteworthy list of customers that included several governors and even kings. To some candle making was a lowly work because the necessary tallow had to be gathered daily from slaughter shops. Agar's father used mostly camel tallow though Jews considered the camel unclean, but to the other assortment of Jerusalem residents the meat was cheap and plentiful. Regularly the young Agar Barshoman fetched open buckets of the strong-smelling tallow from slaughter shops where camels were killed and butchered. Because of the stench that accompanied such places the neighborhood was rough; thus, in early life Agar was exposed to the criminal element of his home town.

When Agar was only thirteen his father suddenly became ill and died, and within months all that the family once had was lost and Agar Barshoman took to the mean streets of Jerusalem alone. He was a bright youth and very quickly learned the basics of first begging and then thievery. Once however Agar got caught stealing the purse of a nomad tribesman and paid the price, the first finger of his right hand. It taught Agar a valuable lesson; there are many ways to steal a man's purse and a lying tongue is quicker than a maimed hand.

Agar Barshoman shrugged nonchalantly and spoke as if he was very bored with the entire subject. He considered faking a yawn then decided against it and said, "My witness is a Roman centurion. He oversaw the crucifixion and will confirm the vial's contents." Again, Agar was lying. He knew however that any Roman could be bribed and if the vial brought a substantial profit Agar would find a centurion to attest his story. Besides, few would dare to call a Roman solder, especially a centurion, a liar to his face. Agar Barshoman congratulated himself on this invented witness; it was a stroke of genius.

Hadid pondered Agar's last words. The Arab was certain Agar was lying, but if a Roman was paid to support his lie, one would be hard pressed to refute it. It was not wise to question a Roman soldier on any matter as they would eagerly display cruelty when impugned. Hadid inhaled deeply from his pipe. His eyes were already beginning to glaze from the effects of the opium. He softly asked, "And the mysteries you spoke of, what is this?"

Agar was ready anticipating the question, "It is very strange," he said soberly while leaning closer to his adversary and lowering his voice so that he was nearly hissing, "The holder of the vial experiences transformation to the past, his own past. You are reminded of every sin committed, every sin!"

The tent erupted with the sound of laughter as Hadid rocked back and rested on his bony elbows gasping, "Surely you do not think me this ignorant, Agar Barshoman. If this were true you would even now still be repenting, yes and in mourning for your own wickedness!" Laughter turned to near hysteria causing the old man to shake and choke. Watching him Agar understood that the opium had reached Hadid's brain and that the bartering was for the present at an end.

Chapter VIII

AGAR BARSHOMAN WALKED AIMLESSLY THROUGH the alley near his home. It was the second evening after the death of the Nazarene and the little man had not slept, had not even been to his room in fact. The weariness that he felt only contributed to his agitated state of mind. Agar had visited two more merchants after leaving the drug-inspired Hadid's tent and the interest in the vial was astounding. Both traders displayed undeniably that they would pay handsomely if Agar could actually deliver the vial and a witness to swear to the content's authenticity. Rather than be pleased with the prospects of fortune so nearly in his grasp, Agar Barshoman was immediately suspicious. Nothing could be this easy he justified, and thus his current frowns. He angrily kicked at a wandering dog that ventured near him never noticing that with its scruffy greasy fur, lowered head and general unkempt look, the animal much resembled Agar himself.

Walking past the building that housed his little room, Agar cursed beneath his breath and shot a dirty look at the inn's rear door. Since the time he first touched the vial until present Agar hadn't any peace. He couldn't sleep or even eat, he wasn't comfortable any place he'd been, and found company lacking even among his usual crowd. Something was definitely wrong Agar sensed, but he just couldn't quite put his finger on the reason he felt this way. These were the thoughts he was focused on when suddenly Agar was three feet off the ground.

Agar sucked in his breath and prayed it wasn't his last. Inside he was trembling like a frightened dove while on the outside he became paralyzed with fear. His mouth turned to cotton, and Agar could not force himself to swallow. Though he would have loved to close his eyes he instead stared in wide-eyed terror at the giant that held him. In the darkness Agar felt more than saw the imposing figure before him. The man was huge, at least six and a half feet tall, and was obviously strong as he easily held Agar suspended in mid-air with just one hand. There was something malevolent in his demeanor, and Agar knew that he was to be the recipient.

Agar grabbed up off the ground

"Agar Barshoman?" the monster queried. He hissed the name between clenched teeth as if afraid his seething anger would be unleashed if he were to open his mouth even a fraction. Agar stared into the coal black eyes, watched beads of sweat trickle down the ebony cheeks and chin and knew he must tell this mad stranger whatever he wanted to know.

"No, that is you must be mistaken, Sir," Agar said, his voice quivering.

The huge black man shook Agar like an old rag and as quickly as a viper's strike wrapped the vise-like fingers of his free hand about Agar's throat. Agar thought his windpipe would surely be crushed. "Lie to me and I will rip out your tongue," the giant said matter-of-factly. Agar knew it was not an idle threat.

"Yes," the little Jew barely voiced, "Yes, I am Agar Barshoman." This was not the first time Agar was hesitant to reveal his identity, but it was the first time he thought doing so would be fatal. The black monster only nodded slightly then spoke again.

"I am told you possess a vial. A vial of blood from…" the big man tried but couldn't say more.

Hesitantly Agar answered, "I, I don't know what you…" the finger tightened, and Agar unconsciously licked his lips.

Agar could nearly feel his tongue being pulled from his mouth, "Yes I have it. I have the vial. I'm the one that has it!" The words poured forth unstoppable. Agar sighed.

"Yes of course you do," the fingers were still tight about Agar's throat as the huge man spoke. "I was there," he said.

Agar only thought he had been afraid, now he was terrified. He was there? There where? Of course, Agar knew the man spoke of the crucifixion but why was he there and even so what did it have to do with Agar. Why is my life being crushed from me he wondered? Suddenly Agar remembered: the vial. That must be it this man too had planned to profit from the Nazarene. Is that all Agar thought and slightly relaxed and then feeling bolder offered, "Perhaps we can reach an agreement? Yes? There will be enough for both of us." Agar felt great.

Not only would he be spared but this fellow would be an even better witness than a bribed centurion. No one would dispute this giant's words. Things were starting to change for the better the Jew thought.

But when the black man began to growl like an animal that had been wounded Agar's hopes of peaceful negotiations were shattered. Once more the fingers tightened, and Agar felt sure his life would end.

"I am going to pinch off your evil little head," the giant declared. "You deserve to die horribly."

Agar found himself nodding agreeably at the crazed stranger. His mind cried out, "Do something, say something you idiot, he is going to kill you." Agar just kept nodding yes.

Suddenly, the black man began to tremble. He still looked into the beady eyes of Agar Barshoman, but it was not Agar's eyes that returned his stare. It was the eyes of the Man, Jesus of Nazareth.

On the road to Calvary, a few days earlier, this same black giant was forced by the Roman guard to assist a collapsed Jesus in carrying the heavy cross to Golgotha. As he was made to kneel and shoulder the weight he came face to face, eye to eye with the Christ. Simon from Cyrene would never forget that meeting. Jesus looked at him half apologetically with eyes unlike any Simon had ever seen. His eyes were alive with compassion and love. Jesus never said anything to him, nor did Simon speak but somehow, they had touched deep within and Simon immediately loved Him.

As the African beheld Agar Barshoman tears began to flow down his beautiful ebony face. Slowly he lowered the smaller man and released the hold he had on Agar's neck. "May God forgive you," Simon whispered softly. "May the Father of the Christ forgive you." The giant slowly shook his head then turned and walked away leaving a very shaken Agar Barshoman alone once more.

Agar stood for long minutes staring after the strange man uncertain what exactly had taken place. A shiver rifled through his body and he felt his neck where Simon's fingers had been. Absently he looked at his right hand and the space where his first finger should have been. He ran his tongue over his lips a couple of times and shuddered again. He started his aimless journey again but this time his head was up, and he searched diligently with his eyes for the black shadows of the night.

The vial was the source of his misery he realized and the quicker he was rid of it the better. A cat screeched near him and Agar turned his head in its direction. The bruised muscles of his neck reminded him of only moments earlier when he was so close to death. Tomorrow I will rid myself of this curse he decided: the vial gone, and all will be back to normal. Except for the fact that I'll be rich, he thought. May God forgive me indeed? May He forgive me if I don't get a ransom for my trouble? Feeling good about himself Agar begin to hum. The tune was one he had learned as a child though of course he didn't realize. The song was titled 'A Day of Reckoning'.

Chapter IX

I T WAS THE SAME COOL night air but a different source than that of Agar's that caused Simon Peter to tremble and draw his robe more tightly about himself. They were in the Garden of Gethsemane, he and John the beloved, the very place where Jesus prayed and wept prior to being arrested. Both men were temporarily lost in their own memories of that dreadful night. It was John who spoke at last. "There is something that deeply troubles me, Simon," he spoke softly.

Simon Peter thought to himself, at last John bears his heart to me. From the moment he and Andrew returned to Jerusalem, earlier in the day, Peter sensed the heaviness that covered his friend. For Simon Peter the day had passed far more quickly and with less tension than he could have imagined. Simon and Andrew arrived before mid-day and had gone at once to the small house where the disciples were in hiding. It was the home of a distant relative of Philip's; distant enough they believed to insure their safety for the time being. Peter was none to eager to face his fellow disciples but knew that he must do so. He was surprised by their reception, in truth overwhelmed.

When he first entered the house, Peter was struck with an overbearing feeling of sorrow. The aura of fear too was strongly present, and Simon Peter saw anguish on the faces of his brethren. Again, Simon was reminded of how much a part of them all the Lord had been. The disciples greeted him and Andrew warmly, doting on

Peter like the prodigal son in a parable the Master once had told them. Simon supposed that to his friends he truly was.

James the son of Zebedee faced Peter squarely saying, "Simon, I have said slanderous things about you and I was not justified in doing so. I ask that you forgive me." Peter was deeply moved, he embraced James but found no words to speak. James then said, "We love you Peter. It is good that you are home."

Peter hailed from Bethsaida, a town of Galilee as James well knew but Simon Peter agreed that where his brothers were, he was at home. It was seeing John though that had shaken Peter most of all. The beloved disciple had changed. He was not charged with the boyish exuberance he normally displayed but under the circumstances Peter had expected this to be the case; however, something more than sadness had taken hold of John. When he crossed the room, and embraced the big Galilean, Peter felt John nearly collapse in his arms. John rested in his grasp ignoring the others and wept, deeply wept. After a few minutes, when no one in the room had dry eyes, John and Peter released one another. Then they ate and talked a little of what the future might hold for them, but the look in John's eyes told Peter that they must speak, and they must speak alone.

Peter believed he knew what was bothering his friend and so before John could continue said, "How could I deny the Lord? I have asked myself this question a thousand times and a thousand times I cannot find an answer. John, you know that I loved Jesus. I know that I loved Jesus. Still, I denied Him. It is true that for weeks I couldn't understand the Lord, I still don't really. When it seemed He could have easily avoided Jerusalem, He came. Though He could have incited the crowds to revolt against the priests and elders, He did nothing. John, we could have fought, we could have overthrown even Rome in time; yet, Jesus would not; why? He often spoke of such a kingdom where He would rule with justice and we would be His judges; yet when we had all these things in our grasp Jesus willingly surrendered. I do not understand. I may never understand."

John who had been looking at his friend as he spoke now turned away. "Perhaps the Lord did nothing," John struggled to go on carefully picking his next words, "Because He could do nothing."

There at last it was out. The truth that had eaten away at John since the crucifixion was finally shared with another. The son of Zebedee looked once again into the emerald eyes of Simon Peter. He saw both disbelief and confusion.

"What are you saying John?" Peter asked realizing for the first time the depth of his friend's torment and that it had nothing to do with Peter's own denial.

"I'm saying that maybe, and may God forgive me for saying so, that Jesus was wrong." The words hung in the air like black clouds that they were. The disbelief and confusion in Peter's eyes now turned to shock and even horror.

The big fisherman's bold voice was scarcely audible as he said, "John you don't know what you are saying. You don't believe that any more than I do." It was more a question than a statement. Peter started to rest his arm across John's shoulders then thought better of it and stopped, but he continued speaking, "John my friend, these past few days have been horrible. We are all grieved. You are tired. You don't know what you are saying."

Suddenly John was tired; tired of being the holder of this awful secret. He must make Peter listen. Someone else had to understand. "Simon, listen to me," he begged. "I was there, remember?" John realized the sting these words carried, like salt they would go straight to the wound in Peter's heart. It didn't matter; John had to make Peter listen. The future of the church was at stake.

"Peter, I saw Him hanging from a tree like a slaughtered lamb. Pierced and bleeding, beaten, so swollen, my God, Simon His blood was everywhere." John's voice cracked and suddenly he was sobbing, deep heart-rending sobs that racked his entire frame. Peter wrapped John in his huge arms and held him fast as tears streamed down his own face as well.

Peter and John

"There was nothing," John sobbed, "Nothing I could do. Oh, dear God, Simon they beat Him so, never has a man been beaten like that." Again, John's words were cut off by his pain. "They mocked our Jesus Simon, they spat on Him and laughed. His Mother, she was there, she saw it all. Oh, dear God, she saw it all. I couldn't look at Him." John's voice now coming in short gasps broke again. "I couldn't bring myself to look at Him. He hurt Simon, I know He did. His blood, His precious blood was everywhere; in the streets, on the ground, oh…" John could speak no more. The memory of Jesus' death invoked a pain he could no longer bear. John the beloved cried himself to sleep in the strong arms of Simon Peter his friend.

Simon studied John's features while he rested and noticed how John had changed these last few days. It was the same look he had observed in Andrew, his brother, yesterday; a look of deep sadness yes but a look of maturity also. John had obviously been forced to bear these horrible memories alone knowing that he must portray strength and leadership on the others' behalf. This strength he did not feel and the leadership role he had no desire to own. Simon Peter pitied John and though he was ashamed the more, Peter was glad he had not witnessed the awful scenes the beloved had; scenes that would haunt him forever.

What had John meant when he'd said that Christ was wrong, Simon wondered, "That He could do nothing?" To Peter these words made no sense. Of course, Jesus could have done something; He simply refused, that's all. He gave up His life; they didn't take it from Him. Peter realized he was angry. He was angry at his Lord. I'm the one that denied Jesus yet I'm mad at Him he thought to himself, and for the first time this allowed Peter to understand why he'd denied all knowledge of his dearest friend.

In truth the denial took place weeks ago when Jesus talked of death and how all this nightmare would happen. Peter was angry then and took Christ aside saying, "Not so Lord, you mustn't talk such foolishness. You can't let this happen and neither will we." It was an unforgettable moment to the big fisherman for Jesus was filled with ire and had rebuked Satan aloud and in front of the other disciples. The Lord may have rebuked the devil, but the sting of His words was felt by Simon Peter and it cut him to the heart. From that point on there seemed to be a veil between them but Peter instead of going to Jesus and making peace kept his feelings buried and as a result the hurt did not go away.

John stirred, and Peter returned his thoughts to the beloved disciple. Funny he felt no hurt or jealousy now; only shame, shame and confusion. Peter finally understood the disciples very much depended on Jesus. They left all their pasts behind, businesses, families, religious convictions, everything to follow the Lord. He was their hope, the one shot at fulfilling all their dreams, the chance to leave a mark on society forever, a way to make a difference. Peter smiled recalling his first meeting with Jesus the Nazarene.

He had been working and since the day's catch was small was busy repairing nets when Andrew bounded up breathlessly saying, "Simon, He comes, the One I told you of; the Messiah."

Both turned in the direction of the white robed Man who walked by them without stopping and simply cast words over His shoulder, "Follow Me and I shall make you fishers of men."

He is more arrogant than I am was Simon's first thought but with a bubbling Andrew tugging on his coat the Galilean decided out of curiosity to find out more. Besides, the day was hot, and Simon was the boss, a day off would suit him fine. When they caught up with Jesus He turned to face them and looking Simon squarely in the eye He said, "You Simon Bar Jona shall be called Peter, the rock."

Simon could not mask the look of perplexity and thought to himself, yes and you will be called mad! Jesus smiled then His eyes twinkling as He added, "No doubt you are right." He turned on his heels and walked away leaving Andrew curious and Simon Peter dumbfounded. From that moment on Peter was a disciple following Jesus, learning more about Him, hungry for His every word and loving the Master. They saw Him perform so many wonderful miracles that one could hardly comprehend. He was everything the Messiah was said to be and more, he was a true friend. Peter never felt about another as he cared for the Lord. What could John have meant? Simon considered once again that Jesus was the Son of God; there was nothing He could not do, or was there?

"I'm sorry Simon," John said apologetically having awakened at last.

"Don't be, my brother," Peter replied. "It is I that must apologize to you and to God for ever having left Jesus' side."

John stood then and placed his hands upon Peter's broad shoulders, "You still don't understand do you Simon? Recall these words from the Lord to you: 'Simon, Simon listen to Me. Satan has asked excessively that all of you be given to him that he might shift you like grain. But I have prayed especially for you Peter that your own faith may not fail; and when you yourself have turned again, strengthen and establish your brethren.' Do you remember these words?" Simon Peter did remember them and how strange they had seemed at the time; still he wasn't sure what they meant.

John must have read his mind for he explained, "Peter, if you had not denied our Lord, had you been there for the crucifixion you would have tried to stop it I'm certain of it and we would be in mourning for you along with the Master. Don't you see that Jesus knew this also? Let His words sink more deeply than the shame you feel. He prayed that you would not fail. You have returned Simon Peter for one purpose only; to strengthen the rest of us and to establish the foundation of the remnant of the body. Your work Simon Peter is not finished, nay only begun."

The big fisherman listened to his companion and did indeed let the words sink in, deeply in. For the first time in several lonely hours Peter felt hope. He felt a new strength take charge of him as if a huge weight had been lifted from his back. Then he remembered John's earlier words about Jesus being unable to do anything, about being wrong, he had to know what John was talking about.

"I pray you're right my friend, but what about our Lord being wrong? What did you mean?"

John opened his mouth to speak but was interrupted by an out of breath Philip who appeared suddenly. "Thank God you're both still here," he gasped. "There is news of an auction to be," he paused briefly, inhaling deeply then continued, "To be held day after tomorrow near the temple."

John and Peter exchanged puzzled looks then Peter hotly asked, "What is that to us? Explain yourself."

"The item to be sold," Philip said in a hushed whisper, "Is a vial of blood, blood from the Son of God!"

Chapter X

THE SALE WAS MEANT TO be held secretly, the premise of which was a fallacy anytime in Jerusalem and especially when the city was teeming with the Passover hordes. Agar Barshoman, determined to be rid of the vial's presence, construed the idea of the auction for two reasons. One, it would alleviate all the back alley haggling, secrecies he felt both weary from and felt threatened him. Secondly, the open bidding would offer him the highest price available. There is nothing like confrontational trade to bring out the best of the notable merchants. Besides, Agar was certain that if all went well he would become a regional legend never again to be publicly despised.

Agar Barshoman was not a man who believed in miracles or divine guidance though surely the idea to steal the Nazarene's blood must have been heaven sent. The small Jewish man with ferret-like features could only imagine his life filled with happiness and peace. Days and nights no longer spent scurrying about in a vain attempt to better his day to day welfare and no longer conniving ways to cheat, steal or otherwise deprive another of their property or purse. Agar could not but dream of being treated decently by others, of someone wanting his company, his friendship, nodding at him publicly, smiling as they passed and unafraid to let their fondness show. Ah but now the vial had changed all that. Yes, he would be well paid for the blood of this criminal, the so-called Messiah, and Agar was pleased that his life would never again be the same. He would be respected at last

even if he did buy the status he craved. At least, he reasoned, it was not his blood that made the purchase.

At a number of well-attended inns where the patrons were shocked by almost nothing Agar Barshoman created quite a stir as he told of what he held in his possession. Those that heard instantly reckoned that he was lying, that the only thing Agar possessed was a recently emptied wineskin. Still their personal beliefs did not stop them from making his claims known in whispered telling to nearly everyone they met. Soon most of Jerusalem was abuzz with Agar's secret and of the auction that would offer the vial.

It was the knowledge of such that had prompted the current conversations between the very un-amused Caiaphas and others of the Sanhedrin council. It was also the reason that for the second time recently Simon from Cyrene found himself between two burly soldiers of the temple guard. Under the orders of the high priest he had been arrested and brought before the council where Caiaphas now questioned him, "You were with the Nazarene at Golgotha were you not?"

Simon's eyes were in direct line with Caiaphas' glaze, but he appeared to be looking clear through his interrogator. The huge black man answered with a clear but gentle tone that did not match his bulk, "I was present on the hill, but I was not with the Man."

"Don't mince words with me you infidel!" Caiaphas shrieked. The priest was highly agitated as was apparent by his nervousness and the anger he failed to keep in check. "Do you know who I am?" Now, were you there, or weren't you?"

"I was at Calvary lord high priest," Simon replied answering both queries.

"Then you are a follower of this Jesus?" Caiaphas well knew why Simon had been here, Roman soldiers having forced him to help Jesus carry the cross, but he wanted a public denouncement to be registered from this man's own lips.

Simon was silent only briefly then answered, "I'd never seen Him before that time."

Caiaphas smiled at how deftly the question had been skirted. He decided to cut to the real reason of the arrest. "Having admitted that you consort with criminals, do you also know a man, if he can be called such, named Agar Barshoman?"

A flicker of recognition showed in Simon's dark eyes and Caiaphas knew the answer before the African spoke, "I know him."

With a nod Caiaphas signaled the guard to the left of Simon and brought the head of his spear sharply against the neck of the black man. The blow was hard and sudden causing Simon to lurch forward and fall upon one knee. He raised his left hand and gently touched the gash from which blood was already beginning to flow. Both guards braced themselves for Simon's attack if it came, but when he did nothing and did not rise they exchanged looks of conquerors and smiled. Caiaphas laughed thus allowing the others among the council freedom to do also.

"I warned you, did I not?" Caiaphas offered with mock sincerity. Simon ignored the high priest and remained motionless watching the blood from his neck as it puddled on the floor. "We have heard that Agar Barshoman intends to sell a vial of blood. Blood he claims is from the Son of God. We are also told that it is blood from the Nazarene liar and that you can verify the blood's origin. Let me assure you Simon Cyrene that if these things are true your own life is in jeopardy. Selling an item that is misrepresented is thievery and to claim the item is from God makes the charge blasphemy for which the penalty is death. If you were truly at Calvary, then you know I speak the truth. I will ask you one time only. Cyrene, what is your part in this contemptible hoax?"

Caiaphas stopped pleased with himself; at his skill in resolving these matters. During his tenure as Chief Priest, Jesus had been a constant annoyance often openly defying the council and Caiaphas himself. The Nazarene was an expert at turning phrases and had often swayed the crowds against the Sanhedrin. Caiaphas saw the Rabbi as an abomination, a threat to everything sacred. The sooner His memory was removed the better for all concerned; thus, Caiaphas would stop at nothing to tarnish Jesus' reputation. The quickest way he knew to dissuade followers was to associate death with the Nazarene's name. Let everyone be acutely aware that to bear the name disciple of Jesus meant to bear their own cross.

After a moment Simon stood and said, "Lord high priest, I am a simple man, an honest man and no thief. I was present at the crucifixion only because I was forced to be. Though I suppose I could have left once the cross was in place I did not. I was not held at the site by these men," he said pointing to the solders, "Nor by another other save one. The one you call Jesus."

Members of the Sanhedrin exchanged puzzled looks and murmured among themselves when this was said but Simon Cyrene ignored them and went on, "Trying to explain this now sounds idiotic I realize and may appear to you all that I am a party to the scheme you described, but I only tell you what I myself know to be truth. There was something about this Jesus that I cannot describe; His very look stays with me still..."

"I have heard enough of this nonsense," Caiaphas exclaimed but someone from the council spoke aloud.

"Let him continue," was stated and others assented so the chief priest had no alternative but to let Simon go on. Caiaphas thought, yes of course you want to hear his lies, so your own story will be more palatable, eh Nicodemus?

Simon turned away from Caiaphas and addressed the entire body of elders more directly, "I never met Jesus of Nazareth before that day, but I declare to you all that He knew me."

Nicodemus knew exactly what Simon meant for he too felt the same way when he first met the Lord. Feeling confident that the other council members were supportive Nicodemus replied, "Tell us what you mean Simon of Cyrene. You state that you never met Jesus, yet He knew you. How can this be?"

By now Caiaphas was seething inside. He had already lost momentary control of the interrogation proving that Jesus, even in death, was a nemesis not easily beaten.

"When, beneath the cross I looked into the eyes of the Man, I felt that He read my thoughts, that He somehow understood my heart and soul; that I was forgiven..."

Caiaphas roared, "This is blasphemy. How dare you speak such lies in our presence? I will not hear it! No mere man can forgive no matter who he declares himself to be. This Jesus was an imposter and so my heathen friend are you. You will pay for these remarks I assure you and your companion Agar Barshoman as well."

Caiaphas was ranting like a madman, waving his hands and shouting at the top of his voice. The other members of the Sanhedrin weren't sure what to do. They wanted to hear the black man's story but did not want to become a party to blasphemy. It was Gamaliel, a Pharisee and one of the most highly esteemed Sanhedrin members that made the decision for them, "Caiaphas you are not the only ears offended by remarks of blasphemy, but we have heard only a heathen's thoughts spoken aloud, not statements against our God. Now, we will let him finish his testimony and if you cannot be silent, you are dismissed from these proceedings."

Stunned silence filled the hall and Caiaphas stood facing and waited as an angry father might have for Simon Cyrene to comply. Nicodemus only smiled. Only Gamaliel could have gotten away with these remarks and Nicodemus knew that Caiaphas was beaten. Slowly the chief priest lowered himself into his seat. Gamaliel then too sat and directed Simon to continue by saying, "I apologize for our internal childish squabbling. Please tell us your story." Caiaphas mentally killed the old man with daggers from his eyes.

"It was at Calvary that I saw Agar Barshoman for the first time. After the Nazarene was crucified but before He died, the little man rushed from a crowd of onlookers and held a vial near the body of Jesus. I didn't realize what he was doing and thought perhaps the man was a follower for Jesus looked at him directly. It was not until later, after the Nazarene's death, that I heard about the evil thing Agar Barshoman had done. I stand before you now and declare that I had no part in the act; I never conspired with Agar to commit this sinful deed. But, I must also tell you truthfully that I witnessed his actions and the vial of blood he possesses is, in fact, blood from Jesus called the Christ."

Again, the council was silent until Annas, Caiaphas' father-in-law announced, "Thank you Simon Cyrene, you may go." Simon nodded in the direction of Gamaliel, turned and exited the hall leaving behind many many unanswered questions concerning his own fate, the fate of Agar Barshoman and leaving two drops of his blood upon the stark white floor.

Caiaphas still glared sullenly at the rest, so Annas gave the next command, "Find Agar Barshoman and his vial and bring him here at once. We will reconvene when Agar Barshoman is arrested."

Outside the Sanhedrin chambers Annas stopped and waited for Nicodemus to appear. Upon seeing him emerge from the outer door Annas took his old friend by the arm and hustled him away from the mainstream of the exiting council. "We must speak privately," Annas whispered and immediately Nicodemus stiffened defensively even though he continued in the direction Annas had chosen.

"Is this need to talk so pressing and scandalous that we must behave as guilty conspirators?" Nicodemus asked attempting to lighten the atmosphere of tension.

"You tell me Nicodemus," Annas snapped in return. "I have been told some very troubling things of late."

"As have we all Annas. Please get to the point."

Annas let go of Nicodemus' sleeve and, satisfied that no one was within earshot, stopped walking and turned to face him. The high priest was surprised that Nicodemus was so calm. "Alright, I'll get to the point. What is the relationship you had with Jesus of Nazareth?" Annas nearly spat the words. He had grown weary of even hearing the name, and to be forced to speak it he found most irritating.

Nicodemus had been expecting this confrontation, but he was not prepared to answer to Annas on the basis of the high priest's personal hatred for Jesus. Nicodemus was also weary of hearing the name of his Lord but only because Jesus' name had been coming from lips that despised the name and from the lips of those that never truly knew Him. Defiantly he fixed his stare on Annas and replied, "He was my Lord."

There, it was out at last Nicodemus thought resolved to hide that truth no more. "I loved Him Annas, and I am convinced He was the Messiah."

Annas could not believe his ears. Nicodemus was mad, hopelessly so. There could be no other reason for this admission. "Do you realize the magnitude of your words Nicodemus? Are you so blind that you cannot see what will become of you?"

"I do not care. Does that surprise you Annas? Well, let me shock you further by adding that you are guilty of murder in my eyes, you and all the rest that voted for the crucifixion of the Son of God."

Annas' jaw visibly dropped upon hearing Nicodemus' words. He took a step rearward as if struck, all color draining from his wrinkled old face, "Dear God, you are mad. You cannot mean what you say."

"Oh, I mean it all right and the only reason I can bear to remain on the council at all is to assure that some measure of justice is allotted. Annas look at yourself. Set aside your own selfish motives for one brief moment and examine this travesty for what it truly is. Jesus of Nazareth was no worthier of death than a child. He was innocent Annas, guilty of nothing, and you know it. If not for the ambitions of Caiaphas, and those like him, Jesus would still be alive. He was all that He claimed to be, and we murdered Him. His blood will ever be on our hands Annas. Yours because he was a threat to your position and power, mine because I didn't have the stomach to oppose you."

The declaration poured forth from the bereaved disciple, it was an admission he had until now been unable to voice. Nicodemus, like his friend Joseph of Arimathea, suffered the pangs of guilt and deep remorse following the death of their Lord. Obviously, it was too late to argue for Jesus' life, but Nicodemus avowed that his faith in the teachings of the Rabbi from Galilee would be made known.

Annas' reaction to the speech ranged from shock to disbelief then extreme rage. His only thoughts when Nicodemus finished were to seek Caiaphas' assistance in reining Nicodemus. Annas promised himself that Nicodemus would pay for these words against him and the rest of the Sanhedrin. "Evidently Joseph shares your beliefs? He has refused to return my messages and his glaring absence from the hall attests to his lack of commitment to our God."

"Your god is self, you pious hypocrite," Nicodemus replied angrily, "And as to Joseph's beliefs, ask him; I speak only for myself."

Annas planned a verbal onslaught to chastise Nicodemus as a traitor who had slandered the high priest and the council, but as he started to speak Nicodemus turned his back to Annas and walked

away adding, "I'm sure you find this a more preferable view for discussion, it is the method you excel in."

Nicodemus kept on walking leaving Annas alone to choke on his rebuttal. The council member was a disciple in secret no more and, despite the repercussions Nicodemus knew would come, he was smiling.

Chapter XI

THOMAS CALLED THE TWIN, ONE of the Lord's disciples, nervously watched the man across the room from him. It was not the stranger's stature or mannerisms that aroused Thomas' suspicions nor was it the fact that all the disciples were on edge. What troubled the young disciple was the robe that the man was wearing. It was solid white with a thin blue thread at the sleeves and collar and it unmistakably marked the man as a servant of the high priest. Thomas could only guess what the stranger wanted. He had arrived saying only that he had news of an event that concerned the followers of Jesus of Nazareth, and he must speak with the one called Simon Peter. When Thomas and the others were hesitant to receive him, the man revealed that a vial of Jesus' blood was to be sold at auction and immediately Philip left to find Peter and John. Now waiting with the temple servant and Thomas were Andrew and Simon Zelotes. The other disciples were scattered through the city and its outskirts fearing a trap was being initiated to capture them. Had James the son of Zebedee been present he could have identified the outsider. However, it is doubtful the knowledge would have eased the tension in the room for James had seen the man once before in the garden the night Jesus was arrested. His name was Malchus; he was a bond servant of the high priest Caiaphas.

Normally a bond servant was a freed man that because of loyalty willingly chose to remain in his master's service. Malchus likewise chose to serve the high priest, but not out of devotion to anything but the style of living he'd become accustomed. Besides if one could avoid Caiaphas during one of his maniacal rages the position was palatable and without discomfort. At least that had been the case until a few days earlier when Malchus accompanied the group sent to arrest Jesus of Nazareth. The plan was simple, seize the rebel leader and bring Him to Caiaphas. There was an ample group of soldiers from the temple guard supplied and no one anticipated much of a fight. To make things easier, one of the Rabbi's own followers would assist the arresting party by identifying the Man with a kiss. Everything went as expected. However, you would have thought Judas had been paid for a performance rather than for betrayal because when the party arrived at the Garden, the traitor fell upon Jesus and kissed Him again and again.

The leader of the temple guard asked the Man if He was Jesus of Nazareth. The response was simply, "I AM HE" and suddenly the arresting party found themselves in assorted positions on the ground. At least for Malchus it was only the beginning of a very long night.

Malchus knew his presence disturbed the disciples waiting with him for the big fisherman to arrive. Rightfully so he supposed considering that he worked for Caiaphas who had initiated the actions that resulted in Jesus' demise. The servant wondered if his own life was now doomed, literally having placed himself in the midst of the Teacher's men. Malchus knew that it was very possible that he could become the focus of the disciples' frustrations and anger. They knew Malchus could be a spy, a pawn being used to bring them together for a final onslaught that would wipe them out once and for all. Malchus knew of course that Caiaphas had no idea he was here, nor for that matter did anyone else, but he also knew that the followers of Jesus were not privy to this truth.

Footsteps could be heard outside quickly approaching the house. Everyone in the room held their breath, momentarily frozen in the throes of individual paranoia. Thomas' eyes grew wide in horror as he noticed for the first time that no one had bolted the door. He immediately rose to do so but was too late. The door flew open and

John the beloved entered followed by Philip and lastly by a very angry looking Peter.

When John saw Malchus he grew more ashen than he already was. The disciple immediately recognized the servant from the Garden of Gethsemane and Jesus' arrest. John would never forget the sight of Simon Peter drawing his short-sword and in an attempt to behead the man nearest him he swung narrowly missing save for the man's ear which was severed cleanly and landed unceremoniously at Jesus' feet. John could not believe that this same man now sat almost causally among the Lord's remaining followers. It was the last place on earth he would have expected to see him.

Malchus felt his mouth turn to cotton when Simon Pater walked in. When their eyes met the servant knew that he had made a grave mistake in coming here. Malchus was accustomed to seeing angry, hate-filled eyes seeing that he lived with the high priest Caiaphas. But he never experienced the cold chill of death that draped him when he looked into the eyes of Simon Peter. Sensing the danger, John immediately turned to face his friend and placed both hands against Simon's chest. Philip moved away from them fearing an eruption was imminent and that it would be sudden in coming.

"You are either a man of remarkable courage," Simon said evenly, "Or you are a fool." The words were not meant to intimidate Malchus nor were they a threat as it was clear to all in the room that Peter meant to kill the man.

"Simon, we don't know for certain that he means us any harm," John replied softly.

"But the vial," Philip said and instantly regretted it.

John responded to Philip without taking his eyes off Peter, "We don't know if it is true Philip, nor if this man is responsible."

Malchus' eyes never left Simon Peter either, the entire scene surreal to him as he listened to disciples debate his fate. An all-consuming quietness filled the room. No one dared breathe or even bat an eye. John could feel Peter's body poised like spring steel ready to strike at any moment. The huge chest was rock hard, and John knew that if Peter chose to attack no one would be able to stop him. Silently he prayed.

After what seemed like an eternity Peter relaxed looking away from Malchus and into the eyes of John. The huge fisherman seemed to be reviewing their earlier conversation, considering what the Lord had said, what John had said. Suddenly Peter was weary of the emotions of anger that nearly all his life had bested him. Simon Peter winked. He surprised them all by saying, "Brother if you have come in peace, peace will be accorded you." John visibly relaxed as did the rest save Malchus who distrusted Peter's sudden mood swing.

Malchus didn't realize that the words Jesus spoke to Simon Peter, the last words, were playing in the Galilean's mind, "Simon put away your sword, those that live by the sword will die also by it. Do you not understand that I could ask My Father and He would send legions of angels to rescue me? But if so, how could the scriptures by fulfilled?"

Peter looked intently at the high priest's servant and asked, "Tell us, what is the reason you've come?"

Malchus slowly looked around the room answering as he did so, "A man was arrested today and brought before the council Sanhedrin. He was a black man from Cyrene and was present at the crucif...at the death of the Nazarene. He was charged with conspiring with another to incite the people by auctioning a vial of blood, blood from your Rabbi." Malchus stopped momentarily as the disciples registered their shock with gasps, exchanging anxious glances.

Hurriedly Malchus continued, "The council's concerns were twofold. First, when the auction was to take place and secondly if the blood was actually the blood of Jesus of Nazareth. Simon the Cyrene could not answer questions about the auction but did assure the council that he witnessed another man steal a vial of blood from your Lord."

"Who was this demon of flesh?" Simon Peter wanted to know.

"His name is Agar Barshoman, a local Jew," Malchus said. "The council ordered his arrest."

"And what of the other?" John asked.

"He was released; he had no part in the scheme. It seems he was merely a bystander."

John remembered Simon Cyrene and was relieved the man who

helped Jesus bear His cross was proven innocent. As to this other man, Agar Barshoman, John had no idea who he was.

"Tell me," Simon Peter asked still unnervingly calm, "Where can I find Agar Barshoman?"

"I do not know, truly. I wish that I did."

"The sale; when is it to be held?"

"Day after tomorrow, early, at the residence of Jabal Kaleesh."

"I know the place," said Simon Zelotes quickly, "He is savvy but corrupt official of the proconsul's court. He dabbles in stolen artifacts and antiquities. I have been there with Judas," he lowered his eyes when verbalizing the name of the traitor. "Iscariot told me Jabal was interested in becoming a disciple but..." Simon Zelotes concluded, ashamed that he had obviously been duped.

"I have only one more thing to ask," Peter replied after a moment. "Why tell us these things, and why you?" The questions were not hostile rather purely honest.

Malchus at last smiled, he touched his right ear and said, "I have been blessed beyond my worth. When I heard this most distressing news I realized I must tell the followers of Jesus. I perceive He was a remarkable Man, as are you all. I don't know if you would have me, but I would like to know more about your way."

Peter smiling stood and extended his huge hand to Malchus. When Malchus reached out Peter enveloped the smaller man's hand between his own. "Come my friend, we will walk, and I will tell you everything I can about the Lord."

Outside beneath the stars of heaven and the eyes of God, Peter and Malchus talked more openly together than either could have imagined. Peter told Malchus many of the wonderful things Jesus had done, the personality He exhibited, the things He taught.

"Who was He?" Malchus queried after awhile.

"He was the Son of God," responded Peter.

"Truly?"

"Yes Malchus, truly," Peter knew that this admission glaringly revealed the depth of his sin against the Lord. Would to God that he could ask the Master's forgiveness.

"When He touched me, when He picked my ear from the dirt and placed it against my head, even though I admit I was horrified at first, even in shock I suppose, yet when He looked at me and touched me I felt so very strange."

Peter said nothing and Malchus went on, "Suddenly, I was not afraid any more, I was not in pain, nor was I angry. I was flooded with a calmness that even now I cannot explain." Still Peter was silent. "Later, when I heard about the questioning, about..." Malchus hesitated and Peter supplied the words the servant struggled to say.

"About my refusal to admit I was with Him, that I even knew Him?"

"Yes, that," Malchus said softly then paused briefly before continuing. "It is none of my business, and if you don't care to discuss it, Simon believe me, I understand, but why? I mean in the Garden only moments before you were willing to fight us all to save Him. You alone launched an attack to stave us off and prevent the arrest. You risked your very life. I don't see how then shortly after you could," and this time Malchus finished his question, "Deny the Man you obviously loved enough to die for?"

Peter looked up at the vast expanse of the sky and all the mysteries there that would ever make man wonder. He sighed as if to exhale every trace of the horrible memory of that night. "I was not afraid to die for Him, Malchus as you yourself have pointed out. I don't know what all my feelings were entirely, but I can assure you fear was not among them. For over three years we followed Jesus learning His ways, soaking in His teachings like parched earth the rain, grasping at every word He spoke and trying to make them ours. He taught us of life and love, to hope and live in peace with others and with ourselves as well. Jesus fed us, He clothed us, shared our laughter and wiped away our tears. He literally became our world Malchus, and life without Him was unthinkable. The Lord often spoke of being handed over to worthless man or being beaten and yes even put to death. Most of us thought He was depressed, that He did not actually mean these things would happen. After all, Malchus, He was the Messiah! Didn't the Messiah rule a kingdom, and didn't the scriptures say that the kingdom must be subdued?" Peter paused searching his heart for the honest answer to Malchus' question.

"After the arrest," he paused and looked Malchus square in the eyes to say, "And I am very sorry to have harmed you Malchus. After the arrest I was so disgusted with the Lord's seeming willingness to surrender. I felt that if I started a fight He would be forced to defend Himself. Instead He rebuked me and told me not to interfere with God's plan. Then when someone asked if I were with Him, may God forgive me, but my eyes were only on myself, as always. I was angry, my hope was lost, I felt betrayed." Peter hung his proud head and spoke very quietly. "When asked if I knew Him, I thought to myself, I guess not. After three long years of planning, of investing all my hope in Jesus, believing that He was the Messiah, and now it was over, He was going to die. My brain became dull with the realization that I didn't know Him, I never really knew Him." Again, a long sigh was emitted. Simon concluded, "The words of denial came easily Malchus, they were bitter in my mouth, but they came out all the same."

After a few moments of reflection Malchus replied, "We are not so different Simon Peter, you and me. Both of us are bond servants, both have served loyally; I Caiaphas and you Jesus of Nazareth. In a moment of confusion and frustration you denied your Lord. By coming here tonight with news of the council's plans I too have betrayed Master Caiaphas. What we have done is done, what remains and what will be the measure of our manhood is what we do from this point on. I have seen the way the others look at you Simon Peter," Malchus said gesturing toward the house. "You are their leader. I have seen the way you look too when you speak of Jesus of Nazareth, when you speak of things you learned from Him. Tell me my friend; does three minutes of denial erase three years of loyalty and devotion?"

Peter looked on Malchus with much admiration but did not respond. "And," Malchus continued, "If Jesus had the power to change my life in our brief meeting, with no exchange of words, how much more His virtue has affected thee Simon of Galilee?"

Simon Peter eyed the servant and reflected on words the Lord once used; that little children would lead, that from the mouths of babes would come perfect praise. "Malchus Malchus, you have spoken well, and I thank you. What will you do now? Believe me you are welcome to stay with us."

"Thank you, Simon, but I must return to Caiaphas. I am his

servant as you are Christ's. I will tell him only that I believe the Nazarene was the Messiah and that I seek release from his service for I believe that no man can properly serve two masters." A look of utter amazement was on Simon Peter's face as Malchus half bowed and turning disappeared into the night.

Chapter XII

"SIMON. SIMON WAKE-UP WE HAVE company."

At once Peter was rising and he grabbed for the sword long since discarded. "Who is it John?" he demanded.

"Come," was the beloved disciple's only reply.

Peter shook the sleep from his head and followed John into the main room of the house. By now the other disciples were aware of the disturbance and were beginning to stir. Peter was surprised to see Nicodemus, an old friend and disciple of the Lord, who was accompanied by another man that Simon Peter did not know. Peter warmly greeted the older man while never taking his green eyes from those of the stranger, a feat made easier because the huge black man was as tall as Peter himself.

"Simon Peter," Nicodemus announced, "Everyone, this is Simon Cyrene." The African and the Galilean each held the other's stare then moved closer and firmly grasped forearms in a traditional salute offered between friends.

"I have heard much about you Fisherman," Simon Cyrene said smiling.

"And I you," said Peter returning the smile warmly. "We are all indebted for your services to our Lord."

The black man blinked slowly and gently shook his head from side to side. "It was an honor to be so used, but if I knew then what I know now..." his words trailed off unfinished.

John said, "We have all voiced those same words Friend."

"Ay," echoed Nicodemus softly.

"Come let us sit," John offered, "And tell us why you've come here at this hour."

This was the third morning after the death of Jesus. The sun was still nestled comfortably in the arms of darkness not yet prompted to begin the stretch that would bring daylight over all the earth.

After the men seated themselves Nicodemus began. "This man," gesturing toward Simon Cyrene, "Was brought before the Sanhedrin yesterday on charges that involved a conspiracy to incite riots, charges that might possibly include blasphemy also. Of course, the arrest as well as the charge of conspiracy was perpetrated by Caiaphas and his ungodly companions. It was apparent to the saner members of the council, and we are few, that Simon was innocent and also that Caiaphas' personal hatred for Jesus will not allow him to rest until every trace of the Lord's existence is wiped out. The high priest has become a madman; I warn you that he will stop at nothing."

Peter's thoughts drifted to Malchus and he offered a silent prayer for the servant's safety. Nicodemus went on, "As I have said, Simon was not a party to any plot; however, there is another man that has committed a sin so diabolical that surely he must be a devil."

"Agar Barshoman," Peter stated quietly. Nicodemus and Simon Cyrene exchanged looks of surprise. Briefly John related the story of Malchus and what they knew of this same scheme.

"Then you know of the vial? That it is authentic?" Nicodemus asked.

"Sadly yes," replied John.

"Simon, you say that you saw Agar Barshoman at Golgotha?" Peter asked.

"Yes, and one time since." When the others questioned him with their eyes the African explained. "In the streets I also heard of Agar's wicked plan. I became infuriated though I don't know why exactly. Anyway, I decided that something must be done to prevent this sacrilege. I found out where he lived; not the place but the area. I went there and waited."

"And you found him?" John asked incredulously.

"I found him," Simon answered. Again, the others waited for him to continue. "I found him," Simon repeated, "And when I looked at him I was sickened. I became filled with rage and though it shames me to say so, I intended to kill him."

"But you did not," Nicodemus said softly.

"No. Somehow I was prevented from doing so. At first, I wanted to, believe me. I had his evil throat in my grasp; it would have been so easy to crush the life from him. In fact, I told him that I was going to do so."

"Did he beg for his life?" Andrew queried.

"No in fact he seemed to agree that I was justified."

"Then what stopped you?" snapped Simon Zelotes who seemed angry at everyone of late.

"I'm not sure," the huge man said almost to himself, "But I think that it was the Nazarene." Simon of Cyrene told them of the eyes of Jesus; eyes that he had been unable to forget. He told them of the change he felt deep within himself; that he was not the same man he'd been before touching the cross of Jesus. Unlike the hostile reaction he received yesterday when the council members heard these things this time Simon was among men who understood completely what he meant.

As he finished Peter asked, "Do you think that you could help us to locate Agar Barshoman again?"

"I'm not certain but I know at least what he looks like and the area he frequents."

"Good, then if he is still free we will find him."

"And do what with him?" Andrew asked his brother.

"Prevent him from holding the sale," Peter said flatly. "We will recover the vial and halt this further insult to the Lord."

"And if he refuses to cooperate?" asked another.

"First, we must find him," Peter said not trusting himself to answer the question put to him.

Then Nicodemus offered, "Peter, remember that Caiaphas ordered his arrest. Guards will be seeking Agar Barshoman in the same places you will. You must be careful all of you. Surely you realize that your lives are at stake."

"Yes Nicodemus," John said, "And yours, but did that prevent you from coming here?

"Just the same," Nicodemus brushed the compliment aside, "These two Simons do not blend easily into a crowd alone and together they will stand out like watchtowers."

It was indeed a fact to be considered but Peter dismissed the logic by saying, "Remember the last time the temple guards saw me, I was sobbing like a woman. Even if they do recognize me it could work to our advantage. They certainly will not fear that I pose a threat, and as a decoy I may be able to distract them long enough to prevent Agar's capture. It doesn't matter anyway," Peter declared, "I'm going!" Obviously, there was nothing left to be said.

Chapter XIII

UT AGAR BARSHOMAN WAS NOT sleeping. He could not. The little man sat huddled in the darkness of a Jerusalem back alley despising the night chill, despising his tired body, the lack of sleep that plagued him and especially the vial that brought these troubles upon him. Agar of course, would never admit his own part in his demise, never had, instead finding it more acceptable to curse fate or the gods that worked against him. It was further proof of the smallness of his character. Agar was not by birth deceitful rather it was ingrained within him by repeated thoughts and acts of cheating, stealing and lying. Habits formed and cultivated over an expanse of several years had molded the despicable nature that controlled him. It is of course within the laws of truth that no man can be honest with another when he deceives his own heart first.

Agar's eyes were closed, his thoughts on the events that lay before him, events that would make him a very wealthy man, and thus he did not see the form that deliberately approached him. As the shadow slowly closed to within two feet of Agar an arm inched forward almost imperceptible and, in the starlight afforded the blade of knife could be seen glittering in the otherwise black expanse that enveloped them. Suddenly Agar shrieked, a cry of fear and terror that so startled his assailant that the man fell back. At the same time Agar began to kick wildly at the sprawled form launching an attack so vicious that it left the would-be thief dazed and bleeding. Before the man could gather his own instincts for survival and block the repeated kicks Agar aimed at his head, he was struck unconscious collapsing in the dirt like garbage. Still, this did not stem the blows from raining upon him as the terrified Agar Barshoman continued to assault the inert form.

Finally panting and nearly exhausted Agar realized the fight was over. He stared down at the body of the attacker, then abandoning all pretense of bravado, he turned and ran as fast as he could away from the man. Agar ran until he, at last, could not take another step. Stopping he bent over, rested his hands upon his knees and retched violently. Finished and weak he wiped drool from his mouth with the sleeve of his filthy tunic. Agar began to walk toward the inn where he lived cursing himself for his previous inability to go there. Again, the vial came to mind and again he swore at the memory of it. For all he knew the room had by now been ransacked and the vial no longer there.

Agar constantly peered about on the alert for another would-be assailant. He passed the front of a clothier's shop and stopped abruptly. He looked around to insure no one was present along the street then stepped closer leaning to see inside the building through a barred window in the front. Satisfied that the place was void of anyone to deter him he grabbed one of the iron bars to test its solidity. The bar immediately loosened the mortar at its base old and weak. After a few minutes two of the four bars were lying on the ground at Agar's feet. Stealthily he hoisted his small body up and through the now accessible window landing almost noiselessly on the floor inside. Smiling Agar made his way around the interior until he found a rack of robes that appeared to be his size. Deftly he felt of several before settling on one he believed to be of superior quality by the texture of the fiber. In disgust Agar Barshoman shrugged off his own soiled garment happy to be free of the stench of bile and filth. He held the new robe to his face and breathed in enjoying the smell of its newness. Soon, Agar promised himself, after the sale tomorrow, all my world will be comprised of this same fresh odor. He put the robe on them and smiled again. Satisfied with its feel and his own cleverness, Agar quickly left the shop and continued homeward.

When he arrived at the inn he stood for several moments hidden in the shadows and searched the surroundings for a hint of ambush. When Agar was certain he was safe he cautiously approached the inn's door and slipped inside. Agar made his way quickly to his own room but paused before entering, listening for a moment with his head against the door. Hearing nothing Agar entered the tiny room closing out the world behind him as he shut the door. He hurriedly lit a candle and relaxed a bit when he was satisfied the room was as he left it, though he did not sort through the pile to verify the vial's presence.

"Beautiful," he said aloud noticing the deep purple color of the robe for the first time. "It is the color of royalty, befitting a king." Feeling an overwhelming wave of exhaustion Agar stretched himself out on the small cot. It felt so good to at last lay down and rest his weary body. Yet as tired as he was his eyes refused to close. Agar softly cursed looking at the pile in the corner as he did so. It would be daylight soon and one-day closer to his fortune. If only he could hold on to the vial and to his sanity.

Chapter XIV

WHILE THE OTHERS FINISHED BREAKFAST, Peter motioned silently for John to follow him outside. John believed he knew the reason and his fears were confirmed when Peter said, "I want to know what you meant when we were in the Garden about Jesus being wrong."

"It was nothing Simon; forget it. We have enough to think about with the vial and Agar Barshoman."

"I will forget it when you do," Simon Peter replied, "And from the look of you, you can't."

John looked into Peter's green eyes intently then looking away he said, "It concerns the cross, the death, and Simon I don't want to relive that ever again."

"I understand that John, believe me. Just as I didn't want to keep reliving my denial, but don't you see that I had too. I had to talk about it, think about it until I myself began to make some sense of it. Only then could I let the wounds of my words start to heal. I had to face the truth John and so must you."

John knew Simon was right but couldn't see the significance any longer, at least not right now. "It was nothing," he said again but not convincingly, "Just something Jesus said before He died. Any man, when in the grip and pain of death, says things that don't make sense."

"Yes John, no doubt that's true, but we know that our Lord was not just any man."

John sighed exasperated by Peter's persistence. He looked at Simon again and said, "Jesus said something I couldn't understand, I don't see what it matters now; now that He is gone."

Peter now was the one exasperated by John's avoidance of what was troubling him, "John, Jesus said many things we could not understand; still don't and that's not what really matters; I agree. What does matter are the things we do understand."

"What do you mean Simon?"

"I've learned something the last few days that truly excites me," Peter replied. "It started with something Malchus said; even the fact that he was bold enough to come here. Simon Cyrene too is proof; Nicodemus and who knows how many more. In His last hours, John, our Lord touched lives that He would not have reached in any other way. Men that now are followers John, men Jesus never even spoke to. Think about it my friend. Some that never even knew the Lord now are risking their very lives to further His teachings. Don't you see John? This is what Jesus meant for us to do! To never let His message or His memory die. This is the church He often spoke of; these new followers are the kingdom as the Messiah said He would lay claim to. Yes, the Lord said many things we cannot explain, and we may never be able to, but the teachings must be continued. We must share all the things we do understand. John, we must lay the foundation for others to build on; that is what our Lord meant for us; that is our commission."

While Peter was talking the sun steadily climbed to signal a new day had come. Before John could respond to Peter's exhortation they were interrupted by the appearance of Mary Magdalene. The woman who was their friend was obviously quite distraught. Mary was white as a ghost and she was sobbing. Peter put his arm about her and asked, "Mary, Mary what happened? What's wrong?"

"They've taken Him," she wept. "They've taken the body of the Lord."

Peter and John were at once perplexed and angry. "Tell the others," Peter ordered Mary and he and John ran to the tomb where the body of Jesus was supposed to be.

Chapter XV

ABOUT THE TIME PETER AND John arrived at the tomb another part of this drama was unfolding elsewhere in Jerusalem with an equal amount of confusion and concern. In the bedchamber of Caiaphas, a servant shook the chief priest gently. Normally the task of awakening Caiaphas like this would have belonged to Malchus; however, this servant was not Malchus.

"Lord high priest," the servant spoke gently as he continued to roust Caiaphas, "Please, there is a matter of urgency; please wake up."

Caiaphas sat up quickly. Focusing sleep laden eyes on the servant the priest swung his open hand catching the man on the side of his head and toppling him from the platform that held the bed a foot above the marble floor. "How dare you?" Caiaphas spat out, "Have you lost your mind?"

After what had happened to Malchus the servant thought yes, he probably had. But, he was next in line to this role as personal attendant to Caiaphas and to refuse such advancement was unforgiveable. The man stood and brushed his clothes, careful to keep his head bowed and not look at Caiaphas directly.

"What is the meaning of this Malchus?" Caiaphas spoke out of habit and, upon hearing the name of his recently dismissed bondservant pass his lips, he cursed and added, "May the dog eat dung as his portion forever! Now, why did you disturb me?"

"There are men waiting for you, my Lord."

"Men? What men? Explain yourself fool."

"Your father-in-law and others, my lord, I don' know who they are," the servant replied.

"Fetch me my robe then," Caiaphas ordered. "Don't stand there like an idiot!" If only, the servant thought, he still worked in the kitchen attending his former duties. At least the pots and pans did not offend his ears with all their clanging as did Caiaphas' railings. The servant shuddered as he thought of Malchus.

The evening before Malchus returned to the palace of the high priest and asked to speak privately with Caiaphas, but the high priest insisted that Malchus speak before them all. Some Roman soldiers of the temple guard, Annas and several other members of the Sanhedrin as well as household servants were gathered in the dining hall at Caiaphas' request. The main topic of conversation was the infidel Jesus, the Nazarene, and His followers. Caiaphas wanted to destroy them all obviously obsessed with Jesus' effect on the people. It was at this inopportune time that Malchus chose to declare his feelings.

"Very well Malchus," Caiaphas smugly said, "Now that you've interrupted our conversation and our meal state the reason for your absence earlier and your wanton disregard of your duties." Caiaphas was so pleased with himself, with his obvious control of every situation that he chuckled.

Malchus never looked at his feet or wrung his hands or in any manner apologized for the scene; instead he looked Caiaphas directly in eyes and voiced, "I wish to be released from your service."

Caiaphas blanched as those that had been only mildly interested now put down their utensils or wine glasses and focused solely on the high priest and his servant. Even the other servants stopped midstride watching, waiting for the high priest's reaction.

Caiaphas fought to regain his composure. "You what?" The query was less than brilliant and drew smiles from a few guests.

"I want to be released from your service," Malchus said the words again, slowly and distinctly. He never hesitated nor showed any trace of nervousness. You could have heard a feather fall to the floor. Caiaphas was shocked at Malchus' blatant defiance but he was afraid of the servant's control.

"Malchus you bear the mark of a bondservant; do you not?" the priest said at last in reference the hole in he servant's left ear. "No one forced you to do this; it was a decision you yourself made, true?"

"Yes," Malchus answered.

"Yes," Caiaphas confirmed feeling once again that he was in control but wishing he had spoken with Malchus privately. "And now you wish to be released of your promise to serve willingly and you want me to be a party to your broken oath by allowing it to happen?" Caiaphas fell back in his chair, the color in his face changed to white then violent red. All ears were acutely attentive, everyone scarcely breathed. Caiaphas' mind scrambled to make a connection.

Ultimately, he was forced to ask, "Why and what has caused this relapse in your judgement?" The words came forth as a growl from the high priest.

Malchus knew that there was no turning back now. The servant felt a hare amongst jackals; yet, he knew what he must say, and so he spoke; "Jesus of Nazareth is my Lord and I will never be able to forgive you for murdering the Messiah."

Gasps of shock, outrage and disbelief erupted in the room as Malchus finished. Before anyone could move or even realize what was happening Caiaphas jumped from his chair vaulted the table before him spilling wine and scattering bowls of food as he did so and then he attacked the non-combative Malchus. The high priest struck him again and again about the face and head cursing and spitting on the servant acting like a maddened beast. The entire assembly seemed frozen in horror as they watched the spectacle disbelieving. Finally, Caiaphas stood back from his victim panting and weak. Malchus' lips and nose were bleeding from the attack; his eyes were filled with sadness.

"Seize him," Caiaphas commanded. As two soldiers took Malchus by the arms the high priest beckoned to a third and when the man approached Caiaphas whispered to him. The guard looked perplexed at first but whirled about and exited the room.

Caiaphas glared at Malchus and then looked about the room to measure the feelings of his guests. Assured that they were aligned with him the priest turned again to face Malchus. "So, Dog, you are to offer an opinion on my actions, eh? Very well, Malchus you have had your say. Now I will have mine. You have chosen to defy me by publicly declaring yourself to be a follower of the Nazarene, a criminal and enemy of both the council and our own God. You have further committed an unholy act by questioning my decisions and authority."

Caiaphas surveying the room

Caiaphas whispered to the guard to re-enter the dining room. The guard approached the chief priest and handed him the object he had been sent to retrieve. The observers exchanged questioning looks though no one dared to speak. All eyes were riveted on the item Caiaphas held. The high priest continued though his tone changed a little as he mocked the servant before him. "Dear dear Malchus, I have fed and clothed you. I have allowed you to know my kindness and trust. I have loved you. Still you aren't satisfied; you repay my generosity with deceit, betrayal and ingratitude."

Caiaphas stopped only inches from Malchus and smiled benevolently. "And yet, I cannot be angry with you. I only recall the years of faithful service, the fondness between us, eh old friend?" Caiaphas asked suddenly appearing demonic and vile, "Then be free!" He screamed and in one swift motion raised the shears he had been holding. Several reached for their napkins gagging; some rose to run from the room while others just sat immobile; and Malchus for the second time watched his ear fall slowly to the floor at his feet.

Malchus wasn't angry at Caiaphas, he wasn't even too surprised and oddly the pain wasn't overbearing either. As Malchus stared at his ear, the left one, he realized that this time there would be no healer to touch him, to restore the ear to wholeness. Still, he thought inwardly rejoicing, it is good, very good, to be free!

Chapter XVI

CAIAPHAS WAS NOT AN EARLY riser; had never been, thus he stormed angrily into the entry way of his house demanding to know the reason for his interrupted sleep. The servant said Annas was present as was Cleophus and another member of the Council, Staccus who lived with Annas. Caiaphas never had liked the man but tolerated him because of his father-in-law, even though he suspected their friendship was not completely wholesome. "What is the meaning of this?" Caiaphas demanded sharply.

It was Annas who first responded, "Our fears are realized my son," he said. "This fool has failed to prevent the one act that can ruin us." Cleophus stiffened visibly. Normally any man to openly berate him thusly would have been instantly struck down. On this occasion however Annas was right. Cleophus could only bite his tongue for he had no real defense.

"What are you talking about?" the question was put to Annas but Caiaphas' eyes were locked with those of Cleophus.

"I'm talking about the body and tomb of the Nazarene," Annas said. "It's gone!"

"What do you mean; it's gone?" What's gone? Where?"

"The body, the body is gone! How should I know where?"

Caiaphas was not used to this kind of scolding even from Annas. "You forget old man," he hissed, "I am not one of your..." Caiaphas glared at Staccus but Annas interrupted him.

"Nor am I one of your bondservants," the elder spat back; the first mention of his disapproval of last night's scene with Malchus. "You may think yourself untouchable Caiaphas, but I am telling you that we are all in grave danger."

"Danger? Danger of what? From whom? And what about the body?"

Annas threw his hands in the air exasperated and turned away from his son-in-law. Caiaphas looked again at Cleophus and it was clear that he wanted an explanation. Cleophus knew that his career was over if not his life. The only thing he could do now was swallow his pride and work with these Jews in hopes that a solution could be found. The arrogant Roman found the premise distasteful, but not as sour as death. "A short time ago, while my men were diligently guarding the Nazarene's tomb as I ordered them..."

"Hah!" Annas scoffed at this.

Cleophus ignored him and continued. "While they were on guard something happened and when..." Cleophus struggled for the right words. Not finding them he went on, "Suddenly they realized the boulder that sealed the tomb was moved and that the body of Jesus was gone." He finished with a sigh as if the mystery was resolved. Not so.

"What do you mean something happened?" Caiaphas demanded, "When they what?"

"I'll tell you what he can't seem to say," Annas declared glaring at the Roman. "When they woke up from their nap...if they were there at all..."

Cleophus had known that was what Annas believed; what everyone would believe. What's more and what sickened him was that the old goat was probably right! It was absurd that a half dozen Roman soldiers could be overwhelmed by a few fishermen; or that they could not have seen what was happening. Certainly, they must have been absent from their posts or as Annas had indicated deep in slumber. Well, whatever the truth and Cleophus doubted they would ever know it; the guards' neglect of duty would be fatal. The Roman only hoped his own head would not fall among the rest and it was for this reason he offered no defense. Besides, he hadn't any.

Caiaphas looked first at Annas then at Cleophus still unable to grasp a clear picture of what had happened. "The body of the Man is gone," he said flatly more to himself than to them. "Where are the guards now Cleophus?"

"They are waiting outside."

"No doubt developing a universal lie," Annas added.

"Bring them in; we shall hear their story," the chief priest said.

When the six soldiers were gathered, Caiaphas noticed that one of them was all too familiar. Sadly, the high priest recognized a very good friend; Damitry. Damitry had served as a guard in the temple for many years and he had served loyally. Annas too was alarmed at Damitry's presence. The soldier's reputation was flawless, at least had been until now. For the first time the two priests began to doubt that the Romans were absent or sleeping. Damitry was not the sort of man to allow such a lapse of responsibility and it was Damitry that wore the chevrons of rank making him the senior officer of this group.

Caiaphas addressed him directly, "Damitry, what went on to distract you from your duty?" The question was a charge, yet it offered an excuse. Caiaphas and the Roman captain had shared many wine bottles, many stories together, the chief priest did not want to be responsible for his friend's demise.

"Caiaphas, I know this will sound false, but we were not negligent. We were not asleep nor were we distracted."

"Then you just stood by and let the body be taken?" Annas asked mockingly.

Caiaphas silenced him with a look and said to Damitry, "Go on explain to us what happened."

"We were on guard, bored yes I admit but awake; all of us." The other soldiers nodded their assent. "Suddenly, just before dawn the ground around us began to shake. We were all frightened, but we did not flee. The boulder blocking the opening of the tomb started to move, to vibrate and roll aside. I, being nearest to it, placed my hands upon it to hold it fast but to no avail. I then called for the others and those that could stand rushed to help me. Finally, we were all gathered straining with all our might to keep the stone in place, but we could not. Caiaphas, we simply could not halt the boulder from opening!"

Caiaphas opened his mouth to speak but Damitry stopped him by holding up one hand, the palm open. Slowly he raised the other, also open, and as if one the five soldiers behind him did the same. Each man's hands were severely burned. Before anyone could comment Damitry proceeded. "Then the strangest thing of all occurred. As I said, we were struggling to hold the stone in place, but as it slid further opening the tomb a brilliant light burst forth from within. At first, we were blinded but later we could see, and we all did, the unmistakable form of a man. Whether natural man or a god I know not. I only know that I have never seen such glowing whiteness. I could not move; I could not speak. I could only behold this...this glorious light. Caiaphas, you know me. I am not a spiritual man, nor am I taken to drink while on duty. You know that I am as sane as any man and that I do not speak falsely. Caiaphas, I swear to you in all seriousness I believe this Man, this Jesus of Nazareth; truly He was the Son of God!"

Stunned silence greeted Damitry's confession. Annas for once was dumbfounded; Cleophus hoped the lie was good enough to spare them all and Caiaphas was gripped with fear so that he thought his heart would stop. The high priest knew many deceitful men, heard and spread his own share of lies, and was more at home with liars than with honest men. Yet as he stood searching the eyes of his friend Damitry Caiaphas knew without doubt that Damitry was telling them the truth. The chief priest knew what must be done. Caiaphas swallowed hard and turned toward Cleophus unable to look Damitry in the eyes as he issued his commands.

"These men will be given a sum of money; they will tell absolutely no one what we've just heard. Any breach means the death of all including you Cleophus; is that clear? They will write out and sign confessions to the effect that while they were sleeping on watch the disciples of the Nazarene stole the body to perpetuate the nonsense of Him being Messiah. They will say that they were drunk or with a prostitute or whatever, but I want it made clear that the whole thing is a hoax. These men will be issued orders stating that they are being transferred and I want them out of Jerusalem by nightfall. Any compromise, any deviation from these orders and we will go to

Pilate immediately and inform him of your failure to carry out his orders. Further, we will obtain enough witnesses to testify that these men aided the followers and are guilty of treason. Now get out of my sight; all of you."

The meaning was plain to everyone, be a party to deceit or reveal the truth at the cost of your life. The soldiers turned to leave save for Damitry who was frozen in place by the harsh realization that Caiaphas was entirely evil; hopelessly so. The soldier could not believe that any event with such epic proportions could be so easily undermined, so unilaterally sabotaged. "But Caiaphas," he implored, "Do you realize what you're saying?"

Caiaphas whirled about and faced the incredulous man, "I realize that no matter what you think you saw, no matter what you believe to have happened, Jesus of Nazareth is a dead man! And if you so much as breath a word of any of this Damitry you are as well."

At this point Caiaphas admitted for the first time to himself that he really didn't care, even if Jesus was the Messiah, it was too late now, and as long as he could draw another breath the chief priest would fight to destroy even the vaguest memory of the Man of Galilee! Never was a man's heart more filled with darkness than Caiaphas' was then.

Chapter XVII

SIMON ZELOTES WATCHED THE HOUSE from the street, his robe gathered tightly about him, hood up masking his face. His eyes were smoldering embers of anger as he recalled his previous visits here with the dog Judas Iscariot. Even as he thought these things though, somewhere beneath the hurt, Simon yearned to speak with Judas, to find out what had happened to turn him against the Lord, to ask him why? It seemed like an eternity ago now, but Simon recalled when he and Judas travelled together, telling many about the Teacher, praying for the sick and winning followers to the Lord. Jesus sent them out in pairs, Simon accompanied Judas, watched him witness about the Rabbi's ways, saw him rejoice when other responded. Simon knew for certain that Judas Iscariot had once loved the Lord as completely as any of them and it made no sense that he would betray Him.

Somehow Simon felt responsible for perhaps he should have noticed Judas' estrangement. Maybe he had noticed but just never wanted to confront his friend. Simon Zelotes certainly knew of Judas' growing fascination for material things and knew too that Judas had on occasion pilfered small amounts from their collective purse. Rather than accuse him Simon justified his silence by telling himself that Judas was only taking what belonged to him and if his requirements were less than Iscariot's what of that? Now however Simon knew that covering up was as much a sin. If he'd made Judas aware of his guilt perhaps he would even now be alive.

Simon wondered if the others believed him to be a party in the betrayal. Though no one had implied such he and Judas were nearly always together and if Iscariot would have shared his secret with anyone it would have been Simon Zelotes. He had not done so, of course, but Simon still felt a compulsion to prove himself to the rest. It was for this reason that he now watched the home of Jabal Kaleesh, the purported site of the soon to be held auction, in hopes of observing Agar Barshoman and obtaining the vial he had stolen. Simon was aware of the risks. Soldiers were throughout the city, spies also, seeking the whereabouts of Jesus' friends. The disciples knew that very soon an assault would be forthcoming in an attempt to destroy the followers of the Rabbi. Still, if he could stop the sale and retrieve the vial of the Lord's blood, the others would know he was to be trusted.

Thaddeus startled Simon completely when he took hold of his sleeve in the early morning light. So lost in his thoughts Simon hadn't heard Thaddeus approach and he jumped at least a foot. "Scare me to death and my blood will be on your hands," Simon said angrily. Thaddeus only laughed the more.

"What are you doing here?" he asked chuckling.

"I might ask you the same," Zelotes responded defensively.

"I've come for you of course." Then sobering added, "Simon something's come up. Come, we must go."

"I'm not going anywhere until I find the vial and the one who possesses it," Simon declared.

"I understand how you feel Simon but let it go. It doesn't matter now." Thaddeus anticipated Simon's response.

"Doesn't matter? What do you mean: doesn't matter?"

"Easy Simon, easy, the vial matters but something more so. They've somehow taken the Lord's body". Simon Zelotes could not believe his ears but Thaddeus nodded his head assuring his friend it was true, "Peter sent me to find you," he said. "Come, I'll explain along the way."

Chapter XVIII

RAP, RAP RAP. RAP, RAP rap. The visitor abandoned the decorative knocker and began pounding on the door with the side of his fist. Inside the heavy wooden door Joseph of Arimathea crouched trembling as he chewed fiercely on his lower lip. They've come, he thought, they've finally come for me. Absently he wondered what form of torture they had picked for him. Weeping he began to moan, "Not that, please dear God, not that." He cried aloud as he once again recalled the scene at Golgotha.

Hearing a stir within the visitor shouted, "Joseph open the door. Joseph, it is I Nicodemus." A trick thought the terrified shell of a man. They must think me very simple indeed. He whimpered softly and waited. "Joseph, it's me Nicodemus. Please let me in." It couldn't' be Nicodemus, he was probably already dead thought Joseph.

Outside Nicodemus feared the worse, that Joseph was ill, too ill to open the door even or that his mind was by now so tortured that reason had left him. Nicodemus had been unable to speak with his dear friend since the burial. Joseph was an emotional wreck and Nicodemus feared that his own outburst at Annas would further endanger Joseph; thus, he had avoided coming here. Now though everything had changed, and Nicodemus would not leave without seeing him. It came to him, the key to unlocking the barrier between them, "Joseph listen, listen to me. First, we removed the spikes that held His feet and hands. We took His body down and bathed Him in rockrose and laudanum…"

Joseph held his hands over his ears and sobbed deeply. "Nicodemus don't please don't," he cried. "Nicodemus, it is you."

"Yes, my friend," Nicodemus said gently and waited a few minutes more as Joseph gathered himself and unlocked the door. It opened only slightly letting dawn's light spill into the room. Nicodemus entered quickly and not seeing his friend he closed the door and thrust the bolt in place locking it. Nicodemus heard Joseph before he saw him, but in the darkness, could make out only his form. Having been there many times before Nicodemus knew the location of the nearest lamp and went to it without speaking. Nicodemus lit the lamp and turned to greet his friend. As he did so the light illuminated Joseph allowing Nicodemus to view him completely. Instantly Nicodemus choked a scream swallowing a mouthful of bile at the same time.

Nicodemus began to weep whispering over and over, "Oh dear God, my dear God. Joseph. Oh, dear God."

Joseph of Arimathea looked puzzled at Nicodemus' behavior unsure of the reason his friend behaved so strangely. Unable to rid himself of the reoccurring nightmare and thus seeing, time and again, the blood of his Lord clinging to him, Joseph had scrubbed his arms until no flesh remained. Raw meat stared back at Nicodemus; muscle, nerves and sinew exposed by Joseph's anguished cleansings.

"Joseph, Joseph He is gone. There's no need to suffer anymore." Nicodemus sobbed knowing that Joseph did not understand a word of that he was saying. Nicodemus moved toward his friend and gently supported him with an arm around his waist being careful not to touch Joseph's bleeding limbs. "It's okay now Joseph, everything will be fine," he whispered again tears streaming down his face wetting his silver beard.

"He's gone; yes, gone and we buried him," Joseph said more to himself than to his friend.

"No Joseph, I mean His body is gone," Nicodemus stressed. "They say He has risen. Joseph, Jesus has risen!" For the first time Nicodemus noticed a spark of sanity in the listless eyes and so he said again, "He's risen my friend. Jesus has risen!"

Chapter XIX

AGAR BARSHOMAN WATCHED PASSIVELY FROM within the recesses of the crowd. He was hidden in normality, a realm he well knew, exceeded in as a roach thrives in darkness and in filth. No one noticed him, no one spoke to him, nor did any draw comfort by his presence. He was obscure not only here but everywhere, coursing his way through life unseen and thus required to attain no lofty goals, no unreachable heights, or so he believed. Agar fancied himself a loner needing nothing but his own resourcefulness, his cunning to survive. His devil-may-care attitude suited him Agar told himself. It fit him like a tailored robe allowing no room for responsibility or guilt for shirking the same.

"I am my own man," he oft declared; " I come and go as I please and answer to no one and have no master save self." It was a sad statement of Agar's character, a distorted view of what his values were and, as most his boastings were, an elaborate lie. Agar loathed himself. His life, if one could consider it such, was filled with hour on hour of loneliness, of one failed scheme after another, always just missing, always loosing out and always left with his misery to cling to; his hate of self deepening. But not this time he thought; this time he would grasp the ever-elusive golden ring.

Agar's dark round beady little eyes watched as the cross was laid upon the earth. He saw the soldier point to the Nazarene and he viewed the Man as he slowly lay His torn body upon the coarse wooden structure. Each time He moved fresh blood would appear from one of the many wounds He bore; His back, ribs, neck and buttocks lacerated and torn. Agar observed the other criminals' arms were forcibly stretched and held in place as the spikes were driven through their flesh amidst cries of pain and terror. This strange Man merely closed His eyes; extended His limbs willingly and waited for the mallet to fall. And when it fell, though He winced visibly, he did not cry out. So too He offered His feet, one upon the other, meekly. His chest was heaving, no doubt from the trauma of the ordeal and the pain that must have racked His body; still the Nazarene offered no protest. Agar had never witnessed such bravery. It appeared that the Man was above the agony, that He was here yet strangely absent; Man, but not merely so. The two men on either side were begging for mercy, asking God as well as their captors to forgive them and in the same breath cursing both. The soldiers, satisfied that the spikes were deep enough and that they were fast, hoisted the heavy cross to shoulder's height save for the base which drug across the rock soil jolting the Man upon it as they moved it to the hole four feet in depth. Resting only briefly when they reached the spot, the foot of the cross was then inserted, and the soldiers suddenly released their hold, so it fell with a thud. The shock was obviously harsh so that the Nazarene had the air knocked from Him. Before He could recover the soldiers raised the cross again and again let it drop to pack it firmly in place so that it would stand. Among the crowd of onlookers some gasped and even Agar Barshoman winced. A woman, twenty feet to his left, sobbed almost uncontrollably, a frail woman, near shock he guessed. Agar had seen her earlier on the trek from the city of Golgotha as she feverishly attempted to clean up each drop of blood the Nazarene lost along the way. Someone said she was His mother. Darkness fell upon the scene almost imperceptivity, but entirely.

An hour passed then another as Agar Barshoman waited for his opportunity. Others were less patient, wine bottles were produced, the mocking and laughter all but stopped as many were impatient for the evenings festivities to begin. Several were openly disappointed that God had not shown Himself and rescued His so-called Son. Even the guards were disinterested arguing among themselves and casting lots for the Nazarene's few possessions. Agar Barshoman felt confident that his time had come. He briefly glanced around, then satisfied no one was paying him any mind, the little man stepped forward and approached the dying prophet. His eyes were closed but Agar heard His labored breathing, His heaving chest and knew that the Nazarene still lived. He moved the open vial toward Him. Agar was fascinated being so close to someone at death's very door. He looked at the Nazarene closely beginning with His head and saw for the first time the many punctures the thorns from the crude shaped crown had made, marveled at their depth and noticed that His hair was matted with blood.

Agar was surprised to see that the Man's face was very swollen, was covered with deep purple bruises and was contracted by agony. He saw beads of perspiration on the Nazarene's forehead, partially dried spittle on His face and beard, tears slowly coursing down His cheeks. The Man's lips were swollen, split from repeated blows and were also bleeding; there was even a hole beneath the lower lip where a tooth had pierced the skin. The Nazarene's blood flowed across the fingers of Agar's hand as the vial was held in place against the cross.

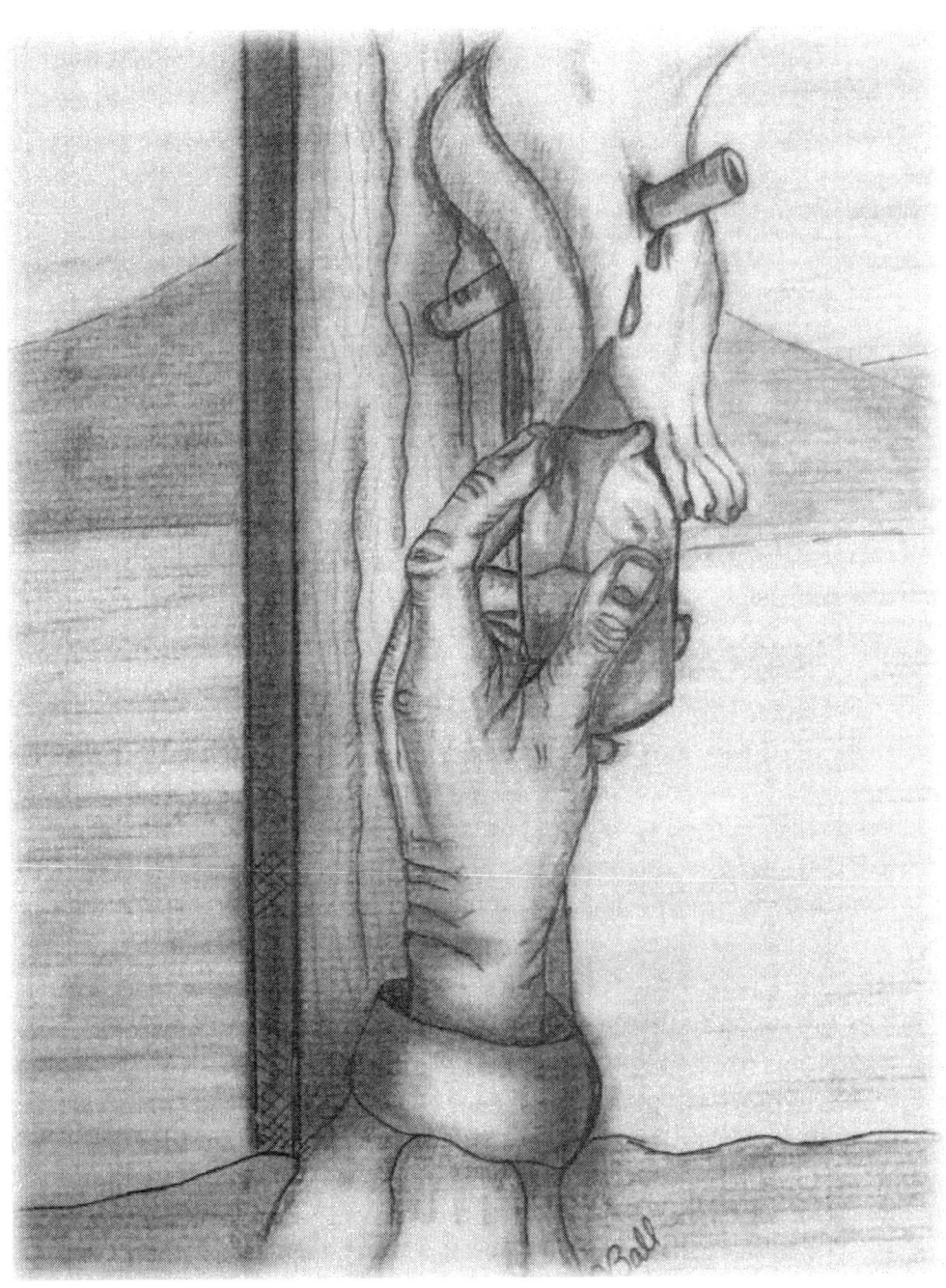

Agar with the Vial at the Cross

What strange twist of fate caused them to be here, Agar wondered. Why were the Rabbi's teachings so different? What made this zealot more unusual than all the rest? Why did the priests and elders fear Him so, enough in fact to murder Him? What caused a Man like this to adhere so strongly to His beliefs that He would die for them? Agar could not begin to understand. The Nazarene was young. It made no sense. Agar looked at the cross and the Man fastened upon it; he looked closely. He saw the placard of charges above the Nazarene's head which read simply 'KING OF THE JEWS', but as Agar peered at the cross itself, beneath the blood writing began to appear. Agar squinted to make the letters out. There were names.

Names in many languages, some he recognized but many he did not. He couldn't understand yet as he looked closer he saw that there were charges beneath the names. The cross was literally covered with them, etched deeply into the wood. There was a name and beneath it – murder, lying, adultery, back biting and on and on, every sin known to man was listed. Below some names only a few, beneath other names there were rows and rows of charges listed.

Agar became engrossed and reached up with his free hand to wipe away some blood to read the words it covered. Suddenly his heart was gripped with fear like he had never known, his eyes grew wide in terror and he tried to cry out but could not. He was so terrified that he screamed and screamed but no sound came forth rather stayed choked in his throat. On the cross was Agar's own name!

Agar Barshoman it read: for lying, cheating, greed, assault, bearing false witness, etc. but the last charge was the most horrible of all. It said, for stealing a vial of blood from the very Son of God. Oh, dear God! Agar wanted to run, he wanted to release the vial and disappear forever, but he was frozen in place. What have I done? What will become of me now? I'm lost, his mind cried out; lost, no one can save me. Agar began to weep uncontrollably, deeply. The tears gushed from his eyes and still he could not move, he could not run. Agar began to repent.

"My greed has done me in; oh, dear God I am so ashamed." He wept. "Please forgive me, I am guilty; forgive me please, have mercy. I should be nailed to this tree not you," Agar cried. "What have I done?

What have I done? My guilt has destroyed your innocence. What can I do? My Lord what can I do?"

Agar Barshoman did not weep because he was trying to save himself, he did not even think to do so, and the sinful little man genuinely meant his words. He was racked with remorse for his wickedness and he repented honestly, unashamedly. When he could weep no more Agar opened his eyes and looked again at the cross of Jesus. He sought the place where he had seen his name written and with a trembling hand Agar reached to wipe the blood away from the spot. His eyes once again opened wide in amazement. He saw his name: Agar Barshoman. It was listed just as before but below it there were no charges! It was as if the blood had blotted them out completely. Agar found a deeper source and new tears streamed down his dirty face. He looked up into the face of the Man called Jesus the Christ whose own eyes now were open resting upon Agar. "My Lord," Agar feebly whispered, "I don't understand."

Jesus smiled and said triumphantly, "It is finished." And from God's throne came a cry that rocked the heavens and the earth as Father watched His Son upon that tree. All hell rejoiced as Satan led the laughter believing he had won; that finally all mankind was lost, all belonged to him.

Agar bolted upright on his bed. A dream? It must have been but how could any dream be so real? Agar turned and felt the cot where his head had been; it was soaked. The tears then, they were shed, they were real enough he thought. The hairs on his neck and arms were on end as they had been while he clung to the cross. The reality of the dream enveloped the little man anew and he shuddered involuntarily. Remembering the scene, he glanced at his hands but there was no blood upon them. Impossible, he thought, I touched it. I know I did. Reason slowly returned to Agar and he began to rationalize the nightmare.

Days since I've slept, exhaustion and stress, the attacks by the black monster and the thief, I haven't eaten much so certainly these things take their toll on a man. How long have I been sleeping? I wonder what time of day it is. I wonder what day it is? The old Agar started to feel in control once more; yet strangely he didn't feel like the old Agar. He refused to think about the vial, did not even dare to look at the corner where it lay hidden and could not shake the overwhelming coldness from his bones. Again, he saw the cross, the eyes of the Man, and the cry of agony from heaven echoed in his mind.

"I called Him Lord!" Agar Barshoman spoke aloud and trembled even more as he attempted to deny the reality of the dream. What a nightmare he told himself. What an imagination. Names and charges, different languages, even my own name was there! Absurd his mind cried out, but suddenly Agar was weeping again. For all the soundness of his logic Agar could not convince himself that it did not take place. He knew that he had not imagined these things. Glaringly his mind's eyes beheld the words: for stealing a vial of blood from the very Son of God! He saw it; it was there emblazoned in his memory. Agar fell back on the cot sobbing and broken.

Agar recalled the night he was caught stealing the Bedowin's purse. He'd been afraid that night but fear soon turned to horror when Agar's angry victim latched onto the frail boyish arm, extracted the gleaming dagger from his belt, then smiling cruelly the Bedowin slowly and deliberately severed the first finger of Agar's hand. Agar Barshoman would never forget the sound made when the finger landed sickeningly in the dirt at their feet. He should have learned a valuable lesson, one would think surely, he did, but had he? Not at all, at least not enough to end his life of crime. Marred forever and for what? For a few shekels? Perhaps? No more. Now though Agar had committed a far graver act of evil and had even laughed about his clever wickedness. The little man knew that this time he would not be so lucky as to get off with only the loss of a finger; nay, death must certainly be the price for theft from God.

Small window with light coming through

Agar opened his puffy eyes and looked at the small opening above the door of the tiny room briefly distracted by dust particles dancing in the air illuminated by the narrow beams of sunlight which filtered into his domestic cubicle. Agar judged it to be near mid-day, not that it mattered in the least for he had no plans or the slightest desire to move from his cot. Imperceptibly Agar Barshoman's hair began to stand on end, and the surface of his skin contracted. Agar realized for the first time that he was not alone in his room! He felt his body stiffen and his breathing almost halt despite his efforts to appear normal. Slowly, agonizingly so, Agar closed his eyes to mere slits and watched the figure across the room from him.

It was obviously a man Agar thought and he is here for the vial. But how did he get in the door was locked and how did he get in unnoticed? Even more frightening was the question of how long had he been here? Agar was not about to wrestle with this stranger for the vial, let him have it and the curse it carried as well. Still, how could he convince this man of his willingness to concede?

Agar believed that even the slightest move could launch the stranger's attack. Agar fought to swallow suddenly remembering the black man's fingers on his throat and when he did force himself to do so he gulped so loud that he was certain the visitor had heard him and would, at any moment, be slashing at him with sword drawn and only one thought, to kill him. Maybe, thought the panicking little man, if I pretend to sleep he'll just steal the vial and go the way he came.

All this speculation ended when the stranger finally spoke, "Agar, Agar Barshoman." It was not a question; the man knew precisely who he was.

That was it then. Agar believed death would be the retribution for his latest sinful deed. The little fellow sighed resigned to face his end and answered softly, "Yes." But then Agar scrambled to resurrect some hope of escape, to salvage enough time to form a plan and so he quickly added, "Yes I know him."

The stranger chuckled softly, "Yes indeed you do, and so do I."

No more deceit Agar decided at hearing these words, besides it wouldn't work. The man knew him, probably hated him, maybe had even for years. I'm finished Agar thought, doomed by my own greed and wickedness. Still the man had laughed. Was it scorn, mockery or was it some shred of decency that all men have deep within them? Perhaps there was a chance after all, maybe...just maybe this man would reason with him?

"Agar Barshoman, I've come for the vial."

Reality hit Agar like a slap in the face. There was no escape, no reason for hope, no deliverance forthcoming. The stranger was here for the vial, the vial of blood Agar had stolen from the very Son of God! No defense could be offered because Agar was hopelessly guilty. Agar Barshoman made a decision; it was time to grow up. Suddenly he wasn't as frightened as before. Agar sat up and opened his eyes. Looking directly at his visitor he said, "Yes, I supposed you had. But before you go grant me a moment's time; that's all I ask, a moment's time."

"For what purpose?" the stranger asked.

Agar inhaled deeply letting the same breath out very slowly. "To prevent you," Agar spoke slowly, "My friend, from becoming a party to the most diabolically evil event ever engaged in by mortal man. A plot instigated in the darkest recesses of my own mind, the seeds of which were no doubt implanted there by Beelzebub himself." Agar could hardly believe his own ears; yet he knew at last that this was the truth. Surprisingly honesty felt good. The little Jew determined to make his confession if allowed and hopefully help this stranger avoid a similar trek into evil.

"I am listening," came the reply.

For the next several hours Agar talked; more than in all his 41 years. He started telling the patient listener about his childhood, his early transgressions, and his tendency to corruption. Agar told him about his missing finger, scheme after wicked scheme, and how sin came to control him. Agar never blamed anyone nor tried to make excuses for his actions, he told the truth and bore the brunt of the guilt alone. Agar then began to tell the stranger of Golgotha, about the vial of blood and the Man to whom it belonged. The little man relived the events of the past few days in vivid detail hiding nothing, cleansing himself by confession, by repenting. When Agar finished his face was stained with tears, the sun had begun to seek its own shelter for the night and the quiet stranger sat on the cot beside him.

When Agar had rested from his much speaking the man asked, "If you could what would you tell the Man from whom the blood was taken?"

Agar thought a moment before responding, "I would tell Him that I was sorry, dreadfully sorry. I would tell Him that I am a greedy sinful man lost in the lust of his own selfish desires. But chiefly I would beg Him to forgive me."

"Agar Barshoman, I AM HE."

His eyes were opened, and Agar fell to the floor at Jesus' feet, tears pooling in the dirt as he kissed them. "My Lord," he wept, "And my God." The tiny room was miraculously filled with a white brightness a thousand candles could not duplicate and so too was Agar Barshoman's heart.

Chapter XX

I T WAS THE FOURTH MORNING after the death of Jesus the Nazarene in Jerusalem and the city was abuzz with news of the open sepulcher. Most of the masses believed that the followers of Jesus staged the removal of the body to enhance their personal standing while besting the elders and high priest of the Sanhedrin in the process. The hoax was the main topic of conversation adding an amusing highlight to an otherwise typical Passover. By now even Pilate was aware of the missing corpse and had launched his own investigation to ascertain the facts. He was angry though not surprised that the Roman guards were unavailable for questioning having been suddenly relocated elsewhere within the vast empire, save for Cleophus the centurion of the temple guard. Cleophus presented signed testimonies stating the soldiers were lax in their duties, had abandoned their posts to sleep off a collective drunk and that the followers of the Nazarene were solely responsible for this now wide-spread rumor of a resurrection. Cleophus informed Pilate that the men of his command were negligent and thus had been subsequently stripped of their rank and privileges and had received assignments in remote areas as punishment. The proconsul informed Cleophus that should any deviation from this version come to light the centurion would be held completely responsible. Rumors were spreading also to the effect that some of Jesus' followers had seen their risen Lord, and though few believed it to be true, it was a tale that made the vial of blood more valuable than ever. So much so in fact that Agar Barshoman's name was being whispered as repeatedly as the Nazarene's.

Chapter XXI

AGAR WALKED BRISKLY INTO THE clothier's and approached its sole occupant wearing the robe he'd stolen from this very site a few days earlier. "May I help you Sir?" the merchant asked politely.

Agar quietly stated that he needed to return the new robe that he was wearing.

"There must be some mistake," the man answered, "The robe is obviously not new. What do you mean you are returning it?"

Agar Barshoman stared at the robe disbelieving his eyes and the fact that until now he hadn't noticed the garment's condition. The shop owner looked at Agar with a quizzical expression that was equal to Agar's. "I don't understand," Agar voiced. "I just don't understand."

"Man, what are you babbling about?" the fellow demanded of his visitor.

"A few nights' past I entered your shop," Agar turned and pointed to the front window where the missing bars had been replaced. "Through there and I stole this very robe from your shop."

The shopkeeper wasn't sure if this was a confession or a question but responded by saying, "Yes, someone did remove the bars from the window as you say, but sir that robe is not one of mine and it certainly is not new. Look at it," he continued, "It is nearly faded white." It was true, the deep burgundy garment was absolutely pale. "Now, if you would like a new one perhaps I can help you, but if not…"

"No, this one is fine," Agar mumbled. "I only thought to pay you for it; that's all."

The merchant shook his head and laughed. "Friend, I see that you are confused. Now if you were the one that tampered with the bars I would thank you not to do so again, though obviously it was time to reset them anyway. As to your robe; surely it was purchased lone ago. Go now; you owe me nothing." Woodenly Agar Barshoman exited the little shop entering the sunlight of what would prove to be for him a very interesting day.

Chapter XXII

SINGLE SOLDIER ENTERED AND STOOD quietly after closing the large door behind him. "Well?" the chief priest Caiaphas snapped.

"Nothing lord priest," the man answered shrugging as he did so.

"That is hardly an answer fool, what do you mean; nothing?"

The soldier was new to the temple guard and bristled at the derogatory comment yet answered evenly, "I mean sir, that he hasn't been found. No one knows where Agar Barshoman is."

Annas dropped his eyes to his lap and Caiaphas cursed loudly. "Get out of here and find him," he said to the guard threateningly. "I want that Dog found." The guard saluted, arm across chest and exited the room glad to be void of the priest's presence.

Caiaphas paced back and forth and cursed the pain that was of late ever present in his burning stomach. "Agar Barshoman will rue the day he was born, or I will kiss the feet of every thief in Jerusalem," the chief priest spat.

"What does it matter now?" Annas asked. "The body's gone, the vial cannot possibly be retrieved before the sale takes place, and Pilate is less than pleased with the explanation of the entire event. We are the laughingstock of all Judea, and Caiaphas, we may well have been responsible for the death of an innocent man."

Caiaphas whirled to face his father-in-law. "You, you are a stoic hypocrite! You act like this is the first time you've considered the

Man's innocence. Listen you old faker, you know as well as I that He was not guilty, but it's just a little late to purify your conscious. If you insist on voicing your doubts, then go home and do so privately."

Annas was not used to this type of verbal abuse, even from Caiaphas, but the elder man was not up to a counter attack. "Very well Caiaphas. You have the necessary appetite for this type of wholesale deception so see to it. As for me, I have had quite enough of Jesus of Nazareth and more than enough of you." The old man turned and left.

Caiaphas said aloud after the outer door was closed once more, "Yes Annas slink away like the serpent you are; I'm better off without your interference anyway." The high priest walked over to his large throne like chair and sat down heavily. He clutched his stomach doubling as he did and cursed again.

Chapter XXIII

JABAL KALEESH STEPPED AWAY FROM the window letting the elaborately ornate drapes close before him. Slowly he shook his large round head from side to side lacing fat stubby fingers on either side of his face while making a soft clicking sound with his tongue. Jabal lowered his arms resting them casually on the large expanse of his midsection. Outside, the normally curious gatherers that were privy to such a clandestine event as the auction had grown into a full-fledged mob. Jabal feared that his immediate superiors would not approve of his participation, howbeit the profit Jabal Kaleesh could realize was far to tempting for him to even consider bowing out. After all, Pilate was aware of Jabal's sideline for the governor himself had purchased, at discount, several antiquities from his underling. Still Pilate clearly did not condone crowds, especially potentially volatile crowds as had collected here.

Jabal turned sullenly toward his dressing quarters to prepare for the sale. He would wear the silver garb. He decided it made him appear ominous and even larger than his 300 plus pounds. Jabal Kaleesh wanted to looked threatening today; the vial must not slip through his grasp. The rotund man wondered if Agar Barshoman had even the vaguest idea of what he possessed, the value of the object. Jabal had heard the purported gossip that made the little purloiner the mastermind of the missing body but dismissed it entirely. Agar was not capable of such cunning and foresight. Jabal Kaleesh believed only that the habitual criminal stumbled onto the idea of stealing the blood originally and that fate had dealt Agar a wining hand as a bonus. Of course, it was not out of the question that some of Jesus' followers were also involved in Agar's scheme, Judas Iscariot betrayed the Man and perhaps another also had the sparkle of greed in his eyes. It didn't matter to Jabal, though personally he doubted the corpse would ever be found, his concern was only for the vial of blood that, with the disappearance of Jesus' body had suddenly become very precious.

Jabal Kaleesh struggled into the brilliant silver robe filling the silken material with his bulk. He smoothed the tunic of embroidered linen beneath it and turned to an immaculate cypress hutch. Opening the second of four large drawers Jabal withdrew several pouches of silver shekels and with them filled the pockets of the robe. From the street a roar erupted, and the merchant assumed the guest of honor had at last arrived. Jabal smiled; honor was not normally a word associated with Agar Barshoman.

In the streets outside the elegant home of Jabal Kaleesh another roar rose from the eager crowd. Several dozen Romans in full battle apparel milled about including the whole of the temple guard. Street hawkers meandered in droves offering everything from sacraments to prostitutes. Their voices could be heard echoing through the noisy gatherers as they called back and forth in wars of open bidding. Chiefly items belonging to Jesus Himself were in demand and thus were most prominently available. A veritable deluge of sandals, tunics, thorn-crowns and even locks of hair could be easily purchased, each coming with a sworn affidavit from the seller that the item was actually worn or from the Rabbi. Dozens of pieces of tattered cloth splattered with the blood from an unfortunate goat or chicken were peddled as remnants of the Master's own final apparel. In truth Jesus could not have worn nor used so many garments or sandals had He been an army of men. Many a merchant cursed his own lack of ingenuity at not thinking of the unholy scandal. Agar Barshoman's stealing of the vial of blood and of offering it at auction was considered a merchandising gem; a stroke of genius. The little thief had become a legend. The carnival atmosphere of the auction boosted the waning

Passover interest so much that many Jerusalem businessmen favored establishing it as an annual event.

Not everyone in attendance stood in the morning air of Jerusalem in approval, however. Many of the true followers of the Christ stood among the curious and greedy pleasure-seekers detesting the unwholesomeness of the affair. Nicodemus was present as was Joseph of Arimathea; the latter's health and sanity restored by the news of his resurrected Lord. New converts too were in attendance, Simon of Cyrene and Malchus among them; men whose lives had been forever altered by brief exchanges with the Rabbi from Galilee. Some thought it odd that the eleven disciples, the leftover band of Jesus' own were absent. Most believed them to be fearful of capture, ascribing the responsibility to them alone for the missing corpse. Lurking in the shadows on the fringe of the spectacle were Caiaphas, Annas and several more of the council Sanhedrin elders awaiting Agar Barshoman, or the culprit disciples so that immediate action could be taken to stop the furtherance of the insults to their leadership.

Jabal Kaleesh, thought to be the foremost candidate to ultimately own the vial, stepped from his home and into the golden sunlight. The crowd exploded in cheers of triumph at seeing him sensing the auction would soon begin. Almost imperceptibly a hush came over the vast group and from the east they began to part leaving a ten-foot swath that led up to the platform where Jabal stood waiting. A little man emerged walking in stunned silence with slightly bowed shoulders hunched. He was freshly bathed, immaculately groomed and wore a well-made faded robe. Whispers asked the obvious question but even those who knew him well would not have easily recognized Agar Barshoman. As he progressed toward the stand the path closed behind him and every eye strained for a better view of the now famous thief. He was the enemy of some, the pity of others and the envy of still more. But everyone pondered, for whatever reason about the vial of the blood of the Nazarene.

Agar Barshoman stepped upon the platform looked only briefly at Jabal Kaleesh and the other buyers he recognized and then said without warning, "There will be no sale this day or any day."

Instantly the curious crowd became the angry mob the soldiers feared. Debris flew at Agar from every direction; those closest to him spitting at his sandaled feet. Behind the little man Jabal Kaleesh, believing extortion Agar's motive shook with anger, his already ruddy complexion deepening rapidly. Raising his fat arms to silence the crowd Jabal moved closer to Agar carefully avoiding the incoming garbage. After a moment the projectiles ceased as did the verbal onslaught and Jabal vocalized the preeminent thought, "What is the meaning of this?" Again, the crowd grew boisterous and again Jabal Kaleesh waited until they were silent. "You have called us all here for a sale and now claim there will be none? I assure you Agar Barshoman you are very wrong." Jabal continued having the full attention of all present, "There will be blood purchased this day and if you do not produce in accordance with your bragging it may very well be yours."

The crowd wildly cheered Jabal's words echoing their full support to carry out the implied threat. Normally Jabal's imposing girth coupled with the violent nature this mob was prone to would have terrified frail little Agar; but this was not the Agar of old and he was strangely unafraid. "I do not have the vial of blood I promised," he simply said.

A roar went up once more. Jabal again silenced them with an upraised arm and asked, "Explain yourself liar; did you ever have such a vial?"

"He did," the voice boomed in answer before Agar's own and Simon Cyrene stepped to the front of the crowd. Agar's eyes grew wide as he looked into the coal black eyes of the African recalling the night the huge black man almost killed him. "He had the vial," Simon said again, "And it was filled with the blood of Jesus of Nazareth."

The mob murmured at Simon's announcement. Those that knew him informed others of his part in the drama and those that didn't know him did not dare ask. Jabal Kaleesh had heard that a black man was witness to Agar's action at Golgotha and assumed this must be him. The angry eyes allowed Jabal to further assume that Agar had likewise betrayed this fellow which, by the look of him, was not a wise thing to do.

"You had such a vial then?" Jabal stated nodding at Agar, "But now you say that you do not?"

"I do not," Agar said quietly still searching the eyes of the Cyrene.

"And do you know where this vial of blood, this vial that recently has become so mysteriously absent can be found?"

Agar knew that this was the moment of truth; his next words could determine the very basis of his life or death. He tore his eyes from Simon and looked above to the blue sky, the downy white clouds, and the brilliant light of the sun. The little former thief smiled and said with all the sincerity he could feel welling up within him, "Right now I believe the vial so precious is in the holy of holies of Almighty God!"

Chapter XXIV

I T WAS THE MOMENT CAIAPHAS had been waiting for, "Blasphemy!"
He shouted bursting through the crowd surrounded as he was by
the temple soldiers. "Blasphemy, arrest the liar," he cried as the
stunned group cleared a way for the priestly entourage.

Several guards reached the platform and two grabbed Agar
Barshoman roughly while two others eyed Simon cautiously but did
not lay hold of him. Arriving at the podium Caiaphas spat covering
Agar's features then stuck him across the face causing a trickle of
blood to appear in the corner of the little man's mouth. "How dare
you speak of anything holy, thief," Caiaphas said. "You know nothing
about honor or truth."

"Nor do you priest," someone with a missing left ear shouted after
which several laughed.

"Let the fellow have his say," another said.

"We'll hear his story; what can it hurt?"

"What say you priest; afraid to let the man speak?" Like shouts
from all portions of the crowd came forth and as quickly as Caiaphas
took control he lost it. Malchus smiled.

Between clenched teeth Caiaphas addressed Agar. "Very well, let
us hear your amusing lies, but I warn you I will not tolerate blasphemy."

"Nor should you," Agar crisply replied delighted to have the
crowd's support. "Jerusalem, foreigners, hear me," Agar began. "Please,
for your own sakes, hear me out. All my life I have been, as those of

you who know me can attest, a liar and a thief. I was not born thus; it is what I became as vainly I sought to satisfy only self. I was a curse to all and to myself, but chiefly I was a curse to God. In my greed I devised a plan, a very simple plan really, to steal the blood of a dying Man, a man who claimed to be the Son of God."

Agar shared with them about the visit from the stranger. "I know you have heard stories about Jesus' missing body. I know that some of you thought me a party to that also, I was not I assure you. And, I am sure many of you believe that the Man's disciples somehow spirited the corpse away. I cannot dissuade you from holding to your own opinions, though would to God I could, but I am here to tell you this one thing. When I fell at the feet of the stranger, when I kissed them yesterday, they bore the marks of the spikes that held Him fast to the tree; a tree He hung on instead of you and instead of me."

Caiaphas had heard enough at last and fell upon the little convert striking him again and again. Mass shock swept the crowd; nobody seemed to know exactly what to do. Near the rear of the assembly Damitry knew what must be done. He moved a step forward when Cleophus gripped his arm and spun the older man to face him. "What are you doing here you fool", he spat. "Don't you know you are risking your life?"

"And yours, eh Cleophus?" Damitry answered. "I know that the body was not stolen. The Man has risen Cleophus. Doesn't that take precedence over personal ambition? Think of the consequences man? He was who he claimed to be. We have been a party to murdering the Son of God and I for one will not stand by while Caiaphas and his sort deny it."

Damitry had made up his mind. He would tell the crowd about the resurrection of Jesus Christ and Cleophus would not sway him. The old soldier turned on his heels to make his way to the platform. Damitry didn't see Cleophus raise the heavy iron bar nor feel the blow from behind that sent him sprawling into unconsciousness. Cleophus drew his dagger from its sheath and bent over the fallen man. He rose, looked about and was satisfied that the brief confrontation had gone unnoticed. Cleophus walked away from the outstretched form of Damitry lying in a pool of his own blood his still quivering tongue in the dirt next to him.

Finally, Simon Cyrene stopped Caiaphas' attack on Agar though he too was quickly surrounded by Roman soldiers. Caiaphas held Agar by the front of his robe shouting, "Where is it? Where is the vial of blood?"

Agar through bloodied lips and with tear filled eyes answered, "I gave it back to the Man I took it from."

"Arrest this infidel," Caiaphas shouted again then strode angrily from the platform.

Agar was held fast by two soldiers but as he was led past Jabal Kaleesh Agar muttered, "I'm sorry to have disappointed you sir, but the blood was never mine to sell. I'm sorry."

Jabal halted the soldiers with an upheld hand. "Agar Barshoman," he said, "I came here today to see the blood of a man hailed as God's Son, to purchase that blood and perhaps enhance my worth somehow in the bargain. I had hoped as well to draw from its virtue, to feel its power if it had any. Agar Barshoman your display here today is testimony that it did indeed. Whoever the visitor of your dream, whoever the possessor of the precious vial, cling to Him Agar for He has given you something that wealth cannot purchase. You've become a man Agar Barshoman, and with this come freedoms you have never known. Each shekel I gain only adds to the bulk of my burden but you my friend have had yours lifted. You my friend have found peace."

Agar was deeply moved by Jabal's words. The little man humbly smiled and said, 'Thank you Jabal Kaleesh, I shall always remember your kindness."

"Thank you Agar Barshoman," Jabal responded, "For allowing me to see things a little more clearly."

As Agar Barshoman was lead away from the platform, his frail body racked with pain and his hands bound tightly behind him, a woman stepped forward. Taking his face between her small hands she kissed his cheek and whispered, "Thank you; thank you." Agar recognized her, knew her tear-stained face at once; she was the Mother of Jesus Christ.

Chapter XXV

THE DISCIPLES OF JESUS CHRIST, some long-time followers and some recent ones, gathered in the home of Nicodemus and shared the exciting news of Jesus' appearance. "You've seen Him then?" Nicodemus asked incredulously.

"Yes," said Peter. "Yes, my old friend; we've seen Him."

"How?" the elder man wanted to know not understanding the resurrection anymore than he'd first understood being born again.

"By the power of God," John answered.

"But what does He say; how does He talk?" asked Joseph of Arimathea.

"He talked just like he always talked," Peter laughed. "And He says that we are to wait until we receive His power; His Spirit."

"Does He forgive us for not declaring our allegiance?" Joseph quizzed softly.

"He forgives," Peter said. "He said that everything that took place was necessary; everything. Indeed; He forgives." The big fisherman turned and looked to another his equal in stature. "And you Simon Cyrene; will you stay with us?"

The huge African truly was one of them now. He'd been arrested along with Agar at the auction but had been released after being sternly warned not to speak of the Christ again and to not interfere in the council's actions regarding the Disciples of Christ. Simon would never forget the conversation he'd had with Agar Barshoman while both were in chains. "It was a brave thing you did today," Simon had offered watching the little man dab the blood from his nose and lips.

"It was a travesty that they were all there because of my wickedness," Agar answered. "But I thank you; and for stopping Caiaphas also. I believe he would have killed me."

"Yes," Simon said softly.

"There was a time I thought the same of you," Agar said to Simon.

"Yes," the black man said again, "I thought I might as well."

"What stopped you, if I may be so bold?"

"His eyes," Simon said reverently. "I cannot forget the Man's eyes."

"Yes," said Agar nodding. "I know precisely what you mean." They were silent, and then Agar asked, "What will happen to us?"

"Who knows save God," responded Simon. "The priest is crazed, and death may be the lot for us all."

Agar nodded in agreement then added, "It matters not; truly. For the first time in my worthless life I am unafraid and not just of death; I am unafraid!" Agar smiled as did Simon Cyrene.

The African's thoughts returned to the present. "No Peter though I thank you for the offer. I have my own calling far from here. I must return to Africa. I want them to know of Jesus of Nazareth."

Peter understood completely and remembered thankfully of another who had knowledge of the Messiah. The Galilean placed his hand warmly on Andrew's shoulder. "Much has happened indeed," Peter replied, "And I believe that everywhere, in every land, people will want to know about our Lord. The events of the past few days will be talked about for generations to come and our Lord's teachings will not fall on deaf ears."

"What about Agar Barshoman; is he still jailed?" asked Simon Zelotes.

"Yes," said Nicodemus. "He has become another focus of Caiaphas' hate."

The African asked, "At the auction when he said he believed the vial of blood to be in the holy of holies of God; what did he mean?"

It was again Nicodemus who answered, "No one can say for certain Simon, but long ago when the temple and its design were established by Moses through God's instruction, Moses was ordered again and again to make the pattern exactly as directed. It is widely believed that the temple, including the holy of holies itself, is an exact replica of heaven and God's throne room."

"Then it is possible that the same rules for sacrifice and the like are also adhered to there, in heaven's holy of holies I mean?" John the beloved queried.

"Possible yes, but I am afraid we cannot know; why do you ask?"

"Well Agar Barshoman stated that he'd given the vial back to the Lord, did he not? If so, why would Christ have need of it?"

"I see what your leading to John, and it's true that blood is the vital requirement for forgiveness; it must be presented by the priest to God personally. But Jesus was not a priest and these things I am afraid we may never know."

Several heads nodded in agreement. Would they ever know the meaning of the last three and half years of their lives? Or even the last few days? Who could explain the huge veil of the temple between the holy of holies being torn from top to bottom when Jesus died? And what about the crucifixion itself? One thing was certain none of them would ever again be the same.

A tear appeared in the corner of Peter's eye when he looked at another recent addition to their fold. It nearly broke his big heart when Peter had first seen what Caiaphas had done to Malchus. The two men had embraced, and Peter wept but Malchus assured his new friend that the ears of one's heart were far more valuable to listen with. Peter was very glad that Malchus was with them.

"There will be persecution," Nicodemus voiced.

"It is only beginning," Philip added.

"But this is a time for victory and celebration," John responded. "My dear friends, our Lord is alive!" There was gladness in all their hearts for the Man that had brought them all together, from many different walks of life, in many different ways, a Man unique and unparallel as any before Him or any that would follow, their Lord, their Savior, their Friend, Jesus was alive!

"John," Peter quizzed his peer, "When we were in Gethsemane and were interrupted, what were you trying to tell me? What was it that bothered you so?"

John thought back to the Lord's words, "Why hast Thou forsaken Me?" The beloved disciple still wasn't certain why Jesus said it or what the question meant, but now it didn't seem to matter. "Never mind Simon Peter," he smiled and answered, "One day soon together we will ask Jesus."

Communion cup

Epilogue

THREE YEARS AFTER THE DEATH and resurrection of Jesus of Nazareth, the Christ, when Caiaphas was chief priest in Jerusalem, a frail sickly little man was brought forth from prison. He had no one to meet him. There was no family and no friends save the unfortunates like himself; fellow followers of the Christ. He squinted in the sun's bright light as he was nearly blind from the years spent in the recesses of the dark and filthy prison. Charged with blasphemy, hated and reviled by the priestly leadership who could not, despite threats, torture and bondage, get this little man to renounce his Lord. Agar Barshoman was led to the outskirts of the city and stoned to death. But even as he faced the bombardment and felt the stones Agar Barshoman was unafraid.

CPSIA information can be obtained
at www.ICGtesting.com
Printed in the USA
LVOW11*0607200318
570339LV00007BA/184/P